LAURENT SEKSIK trained as a doctor, was a radiologist
in a Paris hospital and continues to practise medicine
alongside his work as a writer. Before *The Last Days* (2010)
he published *Les Mauvaises Pensées* (1999, translated into
ten languages), *La Folle Histoire* (2004, awarded the Littré
Prize) and several other books, including a biography of
Albert Einstein. *The Last Days* was a bestseller in France
and has been translated into ten languages. The novel
has been adapted for the stage into a very successful play,
and a film version is currently in production. Seksik lives
and works in Paris.

LAURENT SEKSIK

THE
LAST DAYS

Translated from the French by
André Naffis-Sahely

PUSHKIN PRESS
LONDON

Pushkin Press
71–75 Shelton Street
London WC2H 9JQ

The Last Days first published in French as
Les derniers jours de Stefan Zweig in 2010

Original text © Flammarion, Paris, 2010
English translation © André Naffis-Sahely, 2013
"A Man of Sixty Gives Thanks" translated from the original
poem in German, "Der Sechzigjährige dankt", by Anthea Bell

Published by Pushkin Press in 2013

ISBN 978 1 908968 91 3

This book is supported by the Institut français Royaume-Uni
as part of the Burgess programme (www.frenchbooknews.com)

Set in 10 on 14 Monotype Baskerville
by Tetragon, London
Printed in Great Britain by CPI Group (UK) Ltd, Croydon, CR0 4YY

www.pushkinpress.com

CONTENTS

SEPTEMBER

H E THREW A GLANCE at the beige leather trunk next to the other suitcases in the corridor. He turned to face Mrs Banfield, that dear Margarida Banfield, and reached out to grasp the glass of water she had offered him. He thanked her and drained it in a single gulp. He declined her invitation to inspect the house. He was already acquainted with it. He had loved each of its three tiny rooms and their simple, rustic furniture, the shrill, passionate birdsong outside, as well as how vast the valley looked from the veranda. A few kilometres to the south, the Corcovado and Sugarloaf mountains loomed like monoliths above the islands rising out of the sea—landscapes that hold a special place in the heart of the world.

Goodbye to the fog engulfing the peaks of the Alps, the cold immobile twilight falling on the Danube, the lavish luxury of Viennese hotels, the walks at dusk under the tall chestnut trees in the Waldstein garden, the procession of beautiful women in their silk gowns, the pyromaniac charade of men in black uniforms hungry for the blood and the flesh of the dead. Petrópolis would be the place of new beginnings, the site of all origins, like the dust that man had been born in, and where he was fated to return, the primitive world, virgin and uncharted, a land blessed with order and certainties, a timeless garden where spring reigned forever.

He stood still in front of the trunk in a sort of peaceful hypnosis, as if under a spell. For the first time in months, he felt carefree. He fished inside his jacket's breast pocket for the key to his luggage, which he'd always kept on his person and often fingered like a lucky charm—amidst anxious crowds on platforms or piers while waiting for a train or a boat whose arrival time was shrouded in uncertainty. It worked its magic every time. Touching the key brought him back to the past. A single stroke of its cold metallic surface and he found himself in the horse-drawn carriage he used to ride around the Ring on his way to a premiere at the Burgtheater, or enjoying Schnitzler's company at Meissl & Schadn, or holding a conversation with Rilke in a Nollendorfplatz brasserie.

There would be no going back. Gone were the leisurely moments on the Elisabeth Bridge, the walks along the Hauptallee in the Prater, the sparkling gilding of the Schönbrunn Palace or the sunsets casting their long reddish glow on the banks of the Danube. The night would last for ever.

He turned the key. A crystal-clear light shone out of his open trunk. The sun was rising for a second time on that corner of Brazil. Long since trapped in a dreamless slumber, his spirit experienced a calm elation, while his heart began throbbing, emitting a powerful echo. His heart had started beating again.

He felt a presence behind him, thinking it was the wind. He turned around, convinced that Lotte was there, surveying the scene, finding peace in all that anguish, looking serene and motionless, knowing how to share the solemnity of a moment with him, calm and stoical—reclaiming all she had lost to those days and weeks of endless fear, when they had made their escape, always on the move, the uncertain waits for visas, the interminable queues of faces shedding tears as they pleaded in vain.

All sanctuaries had been desecrated and there were no fixed addresses one might reside at. It had become a roving sort of life, like the exodus of old.

He gazed at her. Her face, which beamed with charm, made him ask himself what right he had to tarnish the radiance of her glances, to consign this youth to the ruins of a beautiful past.

The journey would never end.

Mrs Banfield had prepared some tea, would he care for a cup? He shook his head, but this time his refusal had nothing to do with his sombre reservedness, which led him to decline most invitations. It was a feverish and impatient refusal, but a promising one.

They had finally found a place to lay down their baggage in that autumn of 1941. Many weeks later, they would still be watching the same sunset. For the first time since they'd been in London, they had a fixed address, just a simple address—34 Rua Gonçalves Dias, Petrópolis, Brazil—where they could receive their post and write letters to their loved ones. But they had grown weary of London in the end.

Lotte started speaking to him, with a voice made gentler by her illness, which some days left her gasping for air—her incurable asthma worsened by all that travelling, which occasionally brought her to the brink of asphyxiation. On that morning, her voice did not betray the slightest ailment. Calmly, she said:

"I think we'll be all right. The location is fantastic. I'm certain you'll recover from all your travelling and get back to writing… Perhaps this is where we'll settle into our dotage?"

He scanned his surroundings. The house was plunged in a penumbra. To the right, a narrow corridor opened into a square-shaped bedroom whose floor was covered with an old carpet. Twin beds on iron frames had been pushed together at the back of the room. There was a Bible and an ashtray on the bedside table. Plain white curtains were hanging from nails above the window.

The room gave onto a bathroom, where a couple of towels had been left on the edge of an aged enamel claw-foot tub. The kitchen appeared to be fully equipped. There was an oak table and four straw-backed chairs in the middle of the dining room, as well as a tired-looking leather armchair and a library. There were a few still lifes on the wall. It was a three-room house. They had only given him a six-month lease on the bungalow. In half a year's time, he would have to pack up and find somewhere else to stay. He counted the months with his fingers. Come March, they would be forced to leave. *Raus!* The Zweigs, out on the street! Six months in this nook in the middle of nowhere. A bright, desolate place. Yet did he have the right to complain? His nearest and dearest were presently drowning in an ocean of spilt blood, forced to look for shelter at night, to beg for a hundred dollars to see them through the winter, petitioning anyone with influence for a visa. They were outcasts, the People of the Book, who belonged to the tribe of writers. Taking that into account, the little house in Petrópolis was the most sumptuous of palaces.

He needed to forget his house in Salzburg, banish the memory of that majestic building in Kapuzinerberg, that eighteenth-century hunting lodge whose facade evoked those annexes on the grounds of the Neuschwanstein Castle where the Emperor Franz Josef had played as a child. This is where he'd felt most at ease, closeted behind its thick walls, which guarded over his solitude whether he was writing or in the grips of depression. That noble abode where he'd lived happily.

He had to forget Salzburg. Salzburg didn't exist any more, Salzburg was German. Vienna was German, a province of the Third Reich. Austria was no longer the name of a country.

Austria was a ghost that haunted the minds of the dispersed. A lifeless cadaver. Its funeral had taken place in the Heldenplatz, accompanied by the hoorays of a people cheering their Führer. The man who had come to revive the dreams of yesteryear, to bring the lustre and purity back to a Jewified Vienna. Austria had offered itself to Hitler. Vienna, with its enchanting sights and crystal boulevards, where all hearts opened up, was wallowing in filth, withered by the winds of crime. Vienna was now a witches' sabbath that stretched out its arms to welcome its prodigal son who, born in Braunau am Inn, had recently returned to his native country, where he had been endorsed as king of Berlin and kaiser of Europe by Cardinal Innitzer and hailed by jubilant crowds. It had been three years since the *Anschluss*. The witness accounts of those still trying to escape came thick and fast. They told of hunger, pain and misery. The extermination of Vienna's Jews. The horrors that had unfolded all across Germany were now being played out in quick succession in the small capital, the place where he had spent some of the richest hours of his life.

They had looted the department stores, torched the synagogues, beaten people up in the streets and exposed pious old men in caftans to public persecution. Books had been consigned to the flames—his, as well as Roth's, Hofmannsthal's and Heine's—Jewish children had been expelled from their schools, while Jewish lawyers and journalists had been dispatched to Dachau. They had passed laws forbidding Jews to practise their trade, banning them from public gardens and theatres, from walking the streets most times of day and night, from sitting on public benches, compelling them to register with the authorities, revoking their nationality, stripping them of their wealth and evicting them from their own homes. Lumped together, these laws effectively exiled Jewish families beyond city walls.

11

The Germans were a law-abiding people.

The tragedy played itself out in the city where he'd been born. "History's greatest mass murder," he had prophesied. No one had wanted to believe him. They'd said he'd lost his mind. When he'd packed his bags in 1934, four years before the *Anschluss*, they'd called him a coward. He had gone into self-imposed exile. He had been the first Viennese to do so, the first of many fugitives. "You are suffering from an imaginary emigrant psychosis," Friderike, his ex-wife, had argued. He could have stayed there another four years, like Freud had done, deluding himself that all that evil was merely transitory. However, he had left in 1934, after the Austrian police had searched his home looking for a cache of weapons—weapons in the home of one of pacifism's greatest apologists!

He had felt the winds of change blowing from Germany early on. The hateful speeches, the brutal acts that announced a coming apocalypse to anyone who kept his eyes peeled, as well as those who still paid attention to the meaning of words. He belonged to a race doomed to extinction: *Homo austrico-judaicus*. He had a sixth sense about these things and was well acquainted with history. He had written books on a variety of historical periods, on Mary Stuart and Marie Antoinette, Fouché and Bonaparte, Calvin and Erasmus. Through the prism of past tragedies, he had managed to glimpse into the future and divine the shape of the horrors to come. That war would have little in common with those that came before it.

His cousins and friends who had opted to stay and hadn't wanted to listen to anything he'd had to say, were now in the full throes of misery and hunger. He had been sent accounts of how, from time to time, one of these banished men and women—hungry for fresh air, the perfume of the past and summoned by the light of the sun—would fearlessly venture out into the streets of Vienna, strolling down the Alserstrasse with the hope of enjoying a few moments in the sun. At which point, the accounts continued, some passers-by would recognize the crazed look in his eyes, the fear on his face, and stop him in his tracks, assembling a mob and calling him to order, the new order. Someone in the mob would send a rock hurtling through the air, another would slap his face, encouraging others to hurl themselves at the man in question, raining down blows upon him until blood would start flowing, going at it fiercely; and if an SS officer—who happened to be strolling along the Ring, going up the Florianigasse—ever caught wind of the commotion and came upon the scene, a confused sort of clamour would rise from the growing crowd and all would turn silent as the SS officer pulled a pistol from its holster. The man in the black uniform would aim his weapon, which would glint under the Viennese sun, a bullet would whistle through the air and death would come and resequester that lover of the great outdoors.

This is what a newspaper article he had been sent had had to say:

City authorities in Vienna have decided to cut off all gas supplies to apartments occupied by Jews. The ever rising numbers of suicides by gas have inconvenienced the population and such acts will henceforth be considered breaches of public order.

He breathed the warm air wafting in through the window, which had been left slightly ajar. He contemplated the view of the wide green expanse that the window offered, which extended beyond the city's rooftops. His spirit succumbed to its sweetness. His anxiety subsided. He turned his thoughts to Lotte, as well as

13

to himself. A feeling of shame ran through him, as did one of well-being. He forgot his shame. He smiled shyly at Lotte. He said he shared her sense of relief. That what had won him over during their first visit had been how the living room gave onto the veranda, where a mysteriously invigorating feeling hung in the air. Sitting in the armchair, he felt a certain familiarity with the place.

He bent over the trunk and examined its contents: there were about forty tomes in there. The books had accompanied him on his journey, all the way from Salzburg. He had sworn to bring them out only once his spirit had regained a measure of calm. That moment had finally come.

He pulled the books out, one by one. He slowly perused their covers and ran his fingers over their edges. Then, taking his time, he absent-mindedly—and a little comically—stuck his nose in the pages and sniffed them. These books hadn't seen the light of day since they'd fled their house in Austria. The last fixed address they'd known had been his library in Kapuzinerberg. The passing of time or the crossing of oceans and continents hadn't diminished their perfume. They exuded the scent of his living room in Salzburg. Over the years, the books had become impregnated with its smells: it was a mixture of pine, firewood, autumn leaves, earth after the rain, cigar smoke, apples, old leather, feminine scents and Persian carpets. After the initial enthusiasm and solemnity with which he had opened the first books, he stuck his nose into the other tomes. He inhaled their smell, filling his lungs with it. The pages had kept the fragrances intact. The past was neither dead nor buried. It had been kept alive between the pages of these books. The Gestapo officers had cordoned off the house for a long time, ransacking every nook and cranny, confiscating all the furniture and paintings by great artists, as well as thousands

14

of his other books, but had been unable to make off with that living room's smell. Part of the past had escaped those defilers. The books had preserved the perfumes of life, evoking images of Hofmannsthal smoking his Havana cigars, that poor Joseph Roth savouring his whisky, the revered Sigmund Freud and the aroma his pipe gave off. The memory of all those who had walked through his living room—Franz Werfel and Ernst Weiss, Thomas Mann and Toscanini—had been kept alive. Everyone who was either dead or living in exile would henceforth live on entirely through the smells their presence had once inspired.

When the trunk was finally empty, he felt a touch bemused when face to face with the humble stack of books. Rather pathetically, he groped around the bottom of the box, searching for other books that his eyes hadn't been able to spot. His hand came up empty.

He heard Lotte's voice coming from the veranda. It had the gift of pulling him from the threshold of despair. She had rescued him from depression right from their first meeting in London in 1934, the early days of his exile. Elizabeth Charlotte Altmann's eyes betrayed a penchant for indulgence which his life no longer accorded him. As soon as he'd seen her face, something had become very clear. Instead of the usual bolt of lightning, a blessing had fallen from the heavens and landed right next to him. Hitler could go ahead and invade Europe and become the master of the universe, what did he care? Even today, when nothing seemed to shake him out of his macabre mood, his companion's mere appearance served to instil in him the hope that the world might one day come back to its senses—and that he would live to see it. Neatly arranged, the books took up two shelves. Something to do with how they were aligned annoyed him. He reached for a book that was leaning slightly to one side and straightened it. He took a step back and examined the results, shook his head, grabbed another book and consigned it to a lower shelf. He smiled approvingly, then his face clouded over and he pulled two books from the bottom shelf and placed them on the one above. At which point, he plucked two volumes from the middle of the first shelf and placed each at either end. Then he pulled out another, put it on top of the bookcase, and then put it back. Lotte looked at him without batting an eyelid, though an ironic smile could be detected at the corner of her lips. The process went on for a further ten minutes. Each time he examined the results and seemed satisfied, he went back to work. It was as though he were playing a game of chess with his bookshelf, using the books as pawns. It looked as if the game would never end. Did he have a specific idea of how the books should be arranged? For a moment, Lotte thought her husband had lost his mind. She kept her distance, deciding not to intervene. Who could claim to have hung on to his sanity in those days? A second later, he moved another book, stopped, then turned around, neither looking at her nor uttering a single word. His face was marked by a profound helplessness and untold sadness, dispelling the cheerfulness the task at hand had lent it. He walked around the room in circles, then his shadow melted into the corridor's penumbra. She heard the bedroom door shut and the bedsprings creak under the weight of his body. After that, she heard nothing at all.

His eyes were fixed on the ceiling. He recalled the countless shelves of books that had lined the walls of his house in Salzburg. They looked distinguished, their value was inestimable. Their presence inspired a feeling of tranquillity. When he would turn his head and look out of the window of his lounge in Kapuzinerberg, he could see the Eagle's Nest in Berchtesgaden just across the border, where the man who was menacing humanity made his home. The books had been like a bulwark against him.

The vast legions of his literary masters, a myriad of books covering entire walls, all of which were annotated and whose pages were worn and a little yellowed—works by Tolstoy, Balzac, Dostoevsky, Hölderlin, Schiller, Goethe and Kleist. There was an entire army of autographed books by dear friends of his, such as Rilke, Schnitzler, Freud, Romain Rolland, Jakob Wassermann and Alfred Döblin, all the greatest writers central Europe had to offer, all the talents that had emerged during the interwar years. Then there were his own books, which he kept slightly out of sight, but which were his pride and joy since they were the only fruits his life had borne. Having remained childless, he considered them his own flesh and blood. Then there were the rows of handwritten originals and typescripts. He had owned almost four thousand of them. They ranged from little notes scrawled on bits of paper all the way to letters from Rilke and Goethe's manuscripts. His most prized piece had been Beethoven's journal that genius's record of his youth penned in his own hand, for which he'd paid its weight in gold at the beginning of the 1920s, and which was now part of the booty the Gestapo had confiscated and distributed among various Nazi officials. Yes, Beethoven's manuscript was now in Goering's hands! Goering, who it was said was an admirer of the Jew Zweig's work. He pictured Goering leafing through *Fear*.

Happily, he had been able to safeguard the original score of Mozart's *Das Veilchen*. It had crossed the ocean with him. Mozart's eyes and hands had lain on these pages. How often had he attended recitals of this song, to which Goethe's words had been set? He began to hum that tune and its lyrics. It was the first time he'd sung in ages. The spirit of the old Austria had survived in this place. Mozart watched over him.

His entire life rested upon these shelves. It was framed by its planks.

Nothing was left of the books that he'd kept in his Salzburg house. The people who had written them, those that were still alive, were now scattered throughout the world, fleeing wherever they could, hounded and miserable, penniless and devoid of inspiration, no longer able to tell their stories. Who could start a novel in those times, or weave a more solid and dramatic plot than that which was already being written? Hitler was the author of millions of unsurpassable tragedies. Literature had found its true master.

He pondered over the ridiculous direction his destiny as a writer had taken. Now he only wrote in order to be translated—into English, thanks to that good-hearted Ben Huebsch at Viking Press, and into Portuguese, by Abrahão Koogan. For nearly a decade now, German publishing houses had stopped printing works by Jews—not even Insel Verlag, to whom he'd been steadfastly loyal. He wrote using the language of a people who had outlawed him. Could one be a writer if he weren't read in his own language? Was he still alive even though he was unable to write about his times?

He had been the most widely read author in the world, even though he was convinced that he was far less talented than Thomas Mann, or Schnitzler, or Rilke, or, of course, even Joseph Roth—and he didn't believe a single word of what Freud had said when he'd claimed to prefer his work over Dostoevsky's. He was aware of his weak points, was irked by his novellas' repetitive plots, that limited technique of storytelling that he seemed unable to get away from—or the irremediably tragic way in which his heroes and heroines achieved their destiny either through madness or death. He had sold sixty million books. He had been translated into almost thirty languages, from Russian and Chinese all the way to Sanskrit. His biographies could be found in libraries all over France, Russia, the United States and Argentina. Crowds rushed to see films adapted from his stories. He had written librettos for Richard Strauss. His *Jeremiah* at the Burgtheater had been highly acclaimed. Five hundred theatres had staged productions of his *Volpone*. He had delivered the keynote eulogy in memory of Rilke, his friend, at the Staatstheater in Munich, presided over the opening of the Tolstoy House Museum in Moscow and preached the sermon at Freud's funeral in London. He had encouraged Herman Hesse's first literary efforts, and, were it not for not for his help, Joseph Roth might never have climbed out of the pit of his despair and written *The Radetzky March*. The great Einstein himself had asked to meet with him. He cherished his memory of their dinner at a Berlin restaurant in June 1930, where the scientist had confessed to owning all of his books.

His books haunted him. Their characters—Mrs C. and Dr B., Christine and Ferdinand, Irene, Roland and Edgar—lived on in his spirit. He thought about their fate. The sight of bonfires being kindled in the squares of each German town on that menacing night of 10th May 1933 flashed past his eyes once again. With those crowds huddling around those blazing fires one might have thought one were back in the Middle Ages. The Reich that wanted to last for a thousand years had instead turned the clock back to the year 1000. Once night had fallen and the bonfire was glowing, the ghastly street party had got under way as German youths, cheered on by the crowd, had thrown books into the pyre. The flames had climbed all the way to the sky and the ashes had scattered into the night. The heroes of his novels had been burnt to a crisp.

The sound of Lotte's footsteps in the corridor stopped the train of his dark thoughts in its tracks. Did he want to come and take his seat at the dinner table? Mrs Banfield had asked the kitchen to prepare a Brazilian speciality in their honour. Lotte headed to the window, explaining how one shouldn't sit in the dark. She opened the blinds to their fullest. A wave of light spread through the room. He told Lotte the journey had given him an appetite.

The housekeeper had set the table out on the veranda. In the sky, the seams between night and day had blurred. The air was cooler. Lotte rose from her chair to look for a shawl. They started eating. In her sweet husky voice, she said:

"You know, I think we can finally hang those Rembrandt etchings of yours. They will look splendid in the salon."

Alongside his Mozart score, he had also been able to bring two little etchings signed by the master himself. All of his other Rembrandts, as well as his Klimts, his Schieles, his Munch, his Kokoschkas and his little Renoir, were now undoubtedly hanging on the walls of Goering's house. He contemplated that enchanted, timeless landscape outside, banishing the ghosts that haunted his spirit, if only for a few seconds. The distant echo of military marches was supplanted by the sound of animal calls—monkeys, he assumed. In the eight years since he'd fled from Salzburg, he'd been searching for peace. Yet every time he'd set down his suitcases, the ground had crumbled beneath his feet. Everywhere he went, the war had caught up with him. He hoped it would never get past those hills. He had found the ideal spot for his eternal rest.

"You can finally get down to work on your *Balzac*."

He nodded. The time had come.

Now that he was here, he felt ready. That biography of Balzac he'd begun writing in London was to be his masterpiece. It had to be important, bulky, and would put paid to those criticisms regarding his style. His friends—Klaus Mann, Ernst Weiss, the late lamented Ernst—had never spared him, accusing him of plagiarism and dilettantism. His *Balzac*, however, would command respect; it would be more meticulous than *Marie Antoinette* and more ambitious than *Mary Stuart*. It would stand as a testament to his work ethic and unwavering discipline. It would erase all trace of his mediocre and laughable *Stendhal*. *Balzac* would be his finest achievement. The novelist had been both his mentor and model. Balzac's industriousness and rich abundance of characters fascinated him. He had already written the first part of the book, which dealt with the French writer's life, in London. Yet he wanted to give this book a different spin. He aspired towards an exhaustive examination of Balzac's work, its structure, its essence, something that would encompass the entirety of *The Human Comedy* and remain a useful reference to it. During his five years in London, he had accumulated an incredible wealth of material. Alas, he hadn't been able to find room for it in his baggage. Thousands of files and notes, without which he could not continue his work, were gathering dust in a box on the other side of the world. His friend Ben Huebsch had assured him that this precious package would before long leave London, and that a transatlantic ship would deliver it to Rio soon enough. Though he never usually prayed, he began pleading with the Heavens that the ship might reach safe harbour. The *Balzac* had become his reason for being.

"You're wrong," Lotte said, "you've got nothing to prove. No one stands your equal. Your *Balzac* isn't the only thing you have. Here I am, right by your side. Am I not worth living for?"

He acquiesced. Yes, she was more important to him than anything else. She was worth more than all the books he had written and those yet to come, more than all the novels that had ever been published. She planted a kiss on his hand. Tears streamed down her cheeks. She explained that they were of joy, caused by the happiness she felt at seeing the two of them together in a house far from the reach of men, all alone. Perhaps it had been their destiny all along to be forced onto the path of exile so that they might find one another, far from barbarians and their oaths, sheltered behind a mountain range and buffered by a vast ocean.

He would have loved to believe in destiny, to think that this voyage had been guided by a higher will. Yet he had never believed in God. He felt as though he'd left the keys to his fate in the lock of his house in Salzburg.

*

On the morning of the second day, a beam of light cut through the bedroom blinds and curtains. He partly opened his eyelids. Whereas he had usually needed a few minutes before mustering his energies in the past, he got out of bed immediately. The housekeeper, a friendly young lady whom Mrs Banfield had put at their disposal, made him some coffee, and he drank it sitting on the veranda. Although he had stopped dreaming long ago, it was so bright outside that he seemed to have slipped into reverie.

Lotte got up not long after him. When she came out onto the veranda, the sun cast a beam of light on her. She said she'd been woken up by the sound of birdsong: a primeval sort of choir, the likes of which she'd never heard before. "A tropical symphony," she said, smiling. His thoughts drifted to his friend Toscanini when he'd conducted *Pastoral* in Monte Carlo in 1934. But he didn't linger on these memories. He wanted to make a clean break with the past. Petrópolis had to clear all that dross and nostalgia from his mind.

Lotte had slept well. Her face said it all. Up until that point, the miles they'd travelled had seriously compromised her health. Her condition had worsened in the past few months. The ocean crossing had hollowed her cheeks, damaged her eyesight and chapped her lips. Lotte's heart hadn't coped well with London weather. After they'd left Britain, Lotte's lungs had rejected the New York air during their stopover in that city. That was part of the reason they'd headed farther south. The first time they'd gone to Brazil, a year earlier, the weather in Petrópolis's hilly heights had proved restorative. It was as if they'd gone to the Austrian Alps, to Semmering, Baden or some other spa town.

It had been a long time since her medication had had any effect on her asthma. Every night, around two o'clock in the morning, Stefan had been forced to look on, powerless, as his young wife gasped for air, hovering on the brink of asphyxiation, sitting on the window sill and looking as though she had wanted to breathe all the world's air into her lungs. The continents they'd travelled through, the succession of hotel rooms and the endless uncertainties had accentuated her illness. Just as they had lacked for space throughout their exile, clean air had also been in short supply. Air had been a precious commodity for her. Now they had nowhere left to hide and their finances had run dry. They were even running out of oxygen.

They decided to go out to lunch. Lotte was wearing the beige silk dress she'd purchased in New York the previous month, a few days before they'd boarded the ship for Brazil. They had been living at the Wyndham Hotel on 25th Street, a corner of tranquillity they'd grown very fond of. America had initially looked welcoming. A second life in the New World. They had landed in New York at the end of June 1940, while the Britain they'd left behind was collapsing under the brunt of the German bombing raids. They had enjoyed a few days of happiness, but they had once again had to apply for visas, filling in a great number of forms, asking for references, simply to prove they had the right to exist, even to be there, living in the midst of constant uncertainty and temporary solutions. America hadn't really turned out to be the promised land everyone claimed it was. The more Lotte's asthma worsened, the more their liveliness was sapped. She started having coughing fits. At night, doctors would be at her bedside injecting drugs into her veins. Unfortunately, all that New York air wasn't clean enough for her lungs. Or maybe all the wind stopped at the city limits. Or the breeze that blew over the Hudson was too weak. Or it was all too late and there wasn't any hope left for her. She had contracted that terrible influenza. The fever had made her lose her mind. They had thought she'd been at death's door. He'd spent a whole night nestled by her side on that hospital bed. When she had regained consciousness, she'd heard him mutter some words—but maybe her fever was making her hallucinate? He'd spoken into the abyss, stricken with grief. Her lips had trembled. She'd sworn he'd been addressing the dead, entreating them, telling them about his regrets. He felt remorse for having dragged his wife along on this escapade. His muttering had soothed her. She had fallen asleep lulled by the sound of his voice. After a few days, the fever had calmed down and she no longer wheezed like a coffee pot. Warmth flowed back into her fingertips. She was cured. Those frightening weeks had furnished them with ultimate proof that they didn't belong in New York.

It was a shame as she would have gladly stayed, even though the weather didn't do her any good, even though the lethargy of urban life and car pollution were asphyxiating her. Manhattan was enchanting. At the end of a night's coughing fit, she had seen the city stir and spring to life by the light of dawn through her hotel window. She had gone down to the street. Walking past those skyscrapers had given her vertigo. Everything looked intensely romantic. The streets pulsed with power and a feeling of the unreal. The men and women who crossed her path looked like a new type of human being, one that inspired admiration. In the thick of those crowds, behind those tall walls, she'd imagined herself as the lead actress in a film, a colour film whose images superimposed themselves on the black scenes of that German film. She'd loved losing herself in the crowds on Fifth Avenue at closing time, when employees filed out of their offices—even though she still nursed the terrifying memory of those organized German masses and their outstretched arms. She had strolled through Central Park. The shadows cast by those towers didn't frighten her in the slightest. When a ray of light would slide between two buildings, she would tell herself that the light had fallen from the sky. She would stand still in the middle of the pavement, her head craned up to those heights, her eyes half-shut, wrapped in that celestial brightness. Someone bumped into her. She scurried back to the shadows. She didn't like anyone touching her. The brutal touch of strangers sent the noise of footsteps on the pavement, the shouting of the uniformed mobs, resonating through her mind, which she believed was just as ill as her body. She took a little sidestep and found herself once again in the light, where the air became lighter, where life became lighter.

In New York, Lotte had met up with Eva, her niece, who was the daughter of Manfred, her brother. Eva and Manfred were all that was left of her family. Her mother, uncles, aunts and cousins had chosen to stay in Frankfurt and Katowice, the town in Silesia where Lotte was from and which she had fled in 1933. She hadn't heard from any of them in nearly a year. The courier must not have got through, Stefan had argued.

Lotte had seen her mother staring at her out of Eva's eyes. The resemblance was striking. According to tradition, granddaughters bore their grandmother's names. When Lotte had walked through the streets of Brooklyn with Eva, it had been as if she'd been strolling arm in arm with her mother around the Jewish quarter in Katowice. The department stores' window displays, the restaurant patios and cafés had filled the adolescent with wonder and awe. On seeing the happiness of someone she still thought of as a child, Lotte rediscovered a feeling of insouciance. Eva's peals of laughter effaced the memory of Stefan's bottomless anguish. She forgot about the endless flow of handwritten pages which Stefan produced as he neared the completion of his autobiography, pages that Lotte would have to type out on an old Remington, some of whose keys were broken, working day after day without ever taking a break. She had worn her eyes out trying to understand each of the writer's words, querying the meaning behind every deletion and judging whether his constructions were well balanced. She valued her eyesight highly. All that travelling as well as her illness hadn't prematurely aged them, but the hours she spent reading that manuscript were going to damage them in the long run. Nevertheless, what did she care about her eyesight when all was said and done, so long as she was by his side?

Eva and Lotte had spent one last day together in Manhattan before the couple left for Rio. They had sat down on a restaurant's patio. Three young Americans lunching at a nearby table had come over to ask if the ladies would care to join them. The episode lasted only a few minutes, but it sent a wave of sensual pleasure rippling through them.

They had gone into a little shop on the corner of 42nd Street and Madison Avenue, a tailor's emporium whose window displayed sumptuous dresses at affordable prices. Lotte had hesitated on the threshold and Eva had dragged her in. Lotte needed a dress for her new life in Brazil. On entering the boutique the tailor, a short, corpulent man who was very elegantly attired, had welcomed them as though they'd been oriental princesses. He had brought them some tea and unwrapped entire collections for them.

"You know, people are wrong not to buy any suits and dresses. They're going to need them for V-Day. Because we're going to win, and when I say 'we', I mean the 'People of the Book'. Can the Book-Burning People stand a chance against us?... By the sound of your accent I would say that you're from... Cologne?... Frankfurt and Katowice? Me, I'm from Stuttgart... And when did you leave behind that dear motherland of ours that devours its children? Thirty-Three—you're a real oracle aren't you! I waited until Thirty-Six, and, what's worse, I left my daughter Gilda there. Her husband didn't want to leave. He said the situation couldn't get any worse... what an idiot that Ernst Rosenthal was! My wife had predicted he wouldn't be a good husband, my dear Masha, may her soul rest in peace, she didn't survive the journey. Right after Hermann Flechner got here, having left his son behind in Munich, they were all deported out east. East, as if that were a place fit for Jews!? As soon as the war's over, I'm going to box that Ernst Rosenthal's ears... You know, in Frankfurt I attended my cousin Rivkah's wedding in the big synagogue on Börnestrasse... What's that? Your father was that synagogue's rabbi? What a small... Here we are in August 1941 in New York and you tell me that your grandfather wed Rivkah and Franz Hesen, may his soul rest in peace. Franz met his end when the SA threw him out of a window in May 1933. Is there really no such thing as fate, madam? I haven't even asked you your name madam... Zweig... Do you mean to say you're Mrs Stefan Zweig? Please forgive me, I must sit down, this is all a bit too much for me, first your grandfather officiates at my cousin's wedding, then you tell me all those books my daughter devours were written by your

27

husband. Forgive me, I must seem a little too joyful considering the dark times we live in, but you should be wary of appearances, I'm no fool, I know all too well what the Reich does to our people, but were I to fall into melancholia, I might as well go ahead and close my shop, and then what would I do with the remainder of my days, without my wife and daughter? Nor am I going to spend all day waiting at Ellis Island, since they have shut the great gates, the gates of the mighty Reich and the gates of America. My daughter won't stroll into my shop tomorrow. So I stick to dressmaking, but while that's all well and good, I'm not uncultured, and I can recognize a great writer when I see one, and what's more I've seen a photograph of him in the newspaper. Your husband is a man of rare elegance, please tell him to drop by, you know Max Wurmberg also does menswear, I have pure wool suits that are like the ones the best sewing shops in Berlin used to turn out, not than anyone wants to remember Berlin these days... You know, I only exhibit dresses in my windows because the future belongs to dressmakers, that is if there's any future for dressmakers at all. I prefer not to think about the future too much, that's what fooled Ernst Rosenthal... One day or another, the great Roosevelt is finally going to declare war, I only hope that when he does decide to send his troops over, my little Gilda will still be alive. It's already August 1941, and if he keeps on waiting, I don't know what part of Poland they're going to find her in. It's just that, you see, I would like to be a grandfather, look over here in this box, it's a coat for the baby, with a brocaded velvet exterior, and cotton jersey on the inside. It's for my grandson, look, I've stitched his name on the sleeves, he's going to be called Max, just like me, according to our forefathers' tradition."

He had broken off to search for a dress at the back of the cupboard, saying that it was his favourite, and that he'd set it aside for his daughter, although Gilda would never dare wear it. It was a low-cut red dress that left the back almost naked. Lotte had tried it on, albeit a little reluctantly. The dressmaker had lingered in front of her, on his knees, sticking needles through the cloth and adjusting it. He hadn't spared any compliments when praising her slender figure, her curves, her long legs. He had promised the dress would be ready before their departure.

"You're going to look marvellous, Mrs Zweig, you already look marvellous, look at those hips, those shoulders, you're a dream woman, you deserve the greatest of men."

Then they took their leave.

"You're going to look sublime in your red dress…" Eva had exclaimed.

Lotte hadn't reacted. She walked like a robot, with a faraway look in her eyes.

"On the beach at Copacabana…" Eva had continued.

Lotte couldn't picture herself strolling on a beach. Neither could she imagine her husband walking with her by the edge of the sea. She would undoubtedly never wear that dress.

"You'll be in Brazil in a few days! You don't seem all too happy about it."

Happiness wasn't a word she was accustomed to. Ever since she'd been a teenager, she had thought of joy as vague and out of reach. She wasn't like the other girls. She had known that from an early age. She had the impression that the other girls were happier, more lively and more radiant. She dwelt in shadowy fringes. These days it was easier, people both praised and resented her—after all, she lived in Stefan Zweig's shadow! She would never wear that dress. Her body had always seemed foreign to her. It was a sterile land. Then where did all her hopelessness, which left her feeling lifeless, come from? She'd had a happy and unproblematic childhood. Her father had doted on her, her brother had loved her and her mother had cherished her. They had looked after all her needs. They hadn't denied her anything. Yet nothing but sorrow and suffering emerged from the unreal lands of her childhood. She had always been pervaded by a feeling of defeat. Her respiratory ailment had suited her perfectly as she hadn't needed to adapt to it. She had always felt out of breath, wherever she had happened to be at the time, at home or at school. She had watched her family getting on with the business of living, heard her friends laugh and looked on as the days passed by. She would lock herself in her room, but nothing would happen. She ignored all happiness. She was well acquainted with fear in all its guises. She was afraid of the unknown, of the future, of not doing the right thing, of coming unstuck as well as succeeding; she was also scared of death, of illness, of other people and of fear itself, to the point that even the slightest thing would frighten her to the core. Life had always been like a test, one she found increasingly difficult to succeed at. The grip this misfortune exercised on her had caused her to stumble through those unhappy years. There was no doubt that Lotte had found herself quite at home in her husband's bleak outlook on the world.

"You are the most envied of women, the wife of this century's greatest writer... and you're now the owner of the prettiest dress in Manhattan!"

"Stefan will barely notice the dress. He hardly notices when I'm around."

"But you're the reason he left his wife."

That had just been a pretext... At the time, she must have seemed like a fountain of youth. Witnessing his own energies dissipate, he had hoped to draw on her vigour, not unlike when he had heeded a so-called doctor's advice, who had prescribed him a course of hormones that were supposed to slow down the effects of old age. Alas, against all hope, Lotte had become just another responsibility, yet another burden. As though their life weren't dangerous enough, stifling and shrivelled as it was, marrying her had gifted him with the promise of terrifying nights. What did he feel for her? Nothing but pity.

"Would you prefer to stay in New York with me? He would understand… especially when he's reunited with his books."

"But part of the reason we're going to Petrópolis is for my sake. The town is situated at an altitude of eight hundred metres, he's adamant that it's going to do me a world of good. I can barely breathe here."

"Come, we're going to go all the way to the top of the Empire State Building, where you're going to get a good fill of oxygen."

"I'm going back to the hotel. This walk has tired me out. I didn't take my medication at noon. Promise me we'll spend another day together."

She had hailed a taxi and dropped Eva off. Alone in the car, Lotte had thought about the tailor's story. She had pictured herself getting married in the big synagogue in Frankfurt, instead of that soulless room in Bath, England, where she and Stefan had taken their vows. "*Mazal tov*," she muttered, as if to herself. But there were no practising rabbis left in Germany. Her grandfather had lost his synagogue and was almost certainly dead. There wasn't a single rabbi left in the whole Reich. German synagogues had all been burnt down during the Kristallnacht. The flames had curled up towards the heavens and the stars.

That evening, in their room at the Wyndham Hotel, Stefan had worn the sombre look befitting the dark times they were in. Yet another of his friends, Erwin Rieger, had committed suicide in

Tunis, following in the wake of Ernst Toller, Walter Benjamin and Ernst Weiss. The chasm was widening all around him. The past was being chipped away piece by piece. The tickets to Rio had been purchased. They would board on the morning of 15th August.

Once again, they were on the run. They had fled the Reich, then England, and now the United States. Lotte's health had of course played its part thanks to her weak bronchioles and ailing throat. There had also been the various bureaucratic annoyances to which Stefan had been subjected, being a foreigner from an enemy country. There was also the language barrier. While perfectly fluent, he'd never felt at ease in English. He had also railed against New York's permanent state of frenzy. Everything was chaotic and frivolous.

But there was an altogether different reason for their departure. The real motive was rather shameful—how had her heart hardened to such an extent? Stefan was eager to leave New York because he had found all of Berlin and Vienna in its streets, run into a world of exiles who had lost all their splendour and who limited their talk to tales of woe and complaints. A defeated race wandering amidst the skyscrapers looking for kindred souls to commiserate with. Stefan was leaving New York because he had become a sort of Maecenas there, the person people turned to for support with their visa applications. He was routinely harangued by people wanting money or letters of recommendation. Even though the American authorities had only seen fit to give him a temporary visa, Stefan had been obliged to draft dozens of affidavits, certificates and documents—as well as undertake solemn commitments—just in order to act as a guarantor for a single exile coming out of Germany. He had become a virtual employee of the immigration department. The exiles thought of him as the Messiah. He had sent wads of cash to Roth, that poor Weiss, as well as Bergmann, Fischer, Masereel and Loerke. He'd fought tooth and nail to obtain an Argentinian visa for Landshoff and two Brazilian passports for Fischer. The phone never stopped ringing. People begged for his help, an affidavit, an affidavit, for Scheller and Friedmann, for those who were still waiting in Marseilles or Portbou. An old woman, whose son was living in Warsaw and whom Stefan had promised to help, had kissed his hand. His intercessions had saved four or five of his friends. Hundreds of people were asking for his support. He had become the First Consul of Stateless Jews.

His energies were beginning to flag at the same time as his premonition that the worst was yet to come was growing exponentially. 1941 was going to be the most frightening year in human history, and 1942 would be more frightening still. How could they possibly hope that a stateless writer could obstruct the machinery of death?

The world he had known lay in ruins: the people he had loved were dead; their memory plundered and looted. He had wanted to be a witness, the biographer of humanity's richest hours; he couldn't bring himself to serve as the scribe of a barbaric era. His memory took up too much room, and fear occupied too large a suite in his mind. His writing was fed only by nostalgia. He only wrote about the past.

People ensnared in the mousetrap on the other side of the Atlantic had placed their hopes in his hands. As soon as one survivor was granted a visa thanks to Stefan's efforts, he or she spread the word that Zweig's powers were limitless, that a single appeal on his part had saved an entire family, that the great Zweig will reply, so long as you write to him, Zweig will help you. Dozens of Jews hung around in front of his hotel. Zweig holds out his hand, Zweig shelters and supports, he frees and saves. One day, he will heal all the sick and restore sight to the blind. Enough! He wasn't the Chief Rabbi of all Oppressed Jews, he was simply a writer. He hadn't chosen to be a Jew, neither did he claim to be one. He didn't believe in any god, he never prayed, he condemned Zionism, just like he did all forms of nationalism. Hadn't he already endured enough because of an identity he didn't even associate with? He had lost everything. He wanted them to leave him be! He was fed up of hearing people talk about their miseries, tired of dispensing alms, tired of stories of murders and tortures, of internment camps, of queues of starving people, of legions of exiles, of men who gave themselves over to death, of hearing of souls on the brink of falling apart. He yearned for the peaceful immensity of valleys and plains, for mountains rising from the living earth, the green froth of the sea, the enormousness of the starry sky. He yearned for Brazil.

He had to tell those beggars, lost in their torments, to go and find themselves another Zweig, all enquiries addressed to Stefan Zweig would now be poste restante. They should instead turn to Thomas Mann or Franz Werfel, or Brecht, who still held out hope in Germany, plead their case to Bernanos and Breton, Fierce Fighters of the Free French, they should go knock on Einstein's door, who believed in such a thing as a Jewish nation, yes, those were the heroes and the Righteous.

He had been among the first to flee and was the last of the cowards, the last man, the last Zweig.

*

They walked together down the streets of Petrópolis. Looking into the distance, they could gaze on the slopes of the Serra dos

34

Órgãos, whose impressive bulk cast a sort of serenity on the city, made it feel like it was protected, just like the Corcovado did in Rio. They headed towards the city centre, going through alleyways lined with hydrangeas in bloom. They came across a river where a young boy was fishing with a makeshift rod and where the air was imbued with the smell of herbs. A hummingbird came to rest on an orchid. A monkey's cry rang out from the other side of the river. The hummingbird flew away. They resumed their walk. A wooden bridge spanned the river. A few metres ahead stood an astonishing palace with a crystal and iron façade. Stefan told Lotte about the history of that building, which an aristocrat had given to his wife fifty years earlier. The man had imported all the building materials from France in order to erect a monument to his wife's glory. Hearing those words, Lotte began to dream of how Stefan might one day dedicate one of his books to her—like he had dedicated *The Struggle with the Daemon* to Freud, or *Adepts in Self-Portraiture* to Einstein—a book that would stand as a testament to their love. Rounding a street corner, they came upon a broad boulevard flanked by imposing baroque mansions. They might as well have been in a German city. Had fate brought them here? It was if Germany were stuck to their shoes. Petrópolis had been founded by Dom Pedro I, emperor of Brazil, in the previous century as a summer house for his wife, a scion of... the Hapsburgs. Farmers from the Rhineland had been invited to colonize the land and populate the city. Its neighbourhoods were named after German provinces, while blond children mixed with little mulattoes in the streets. Memories of Germany came crashing down on them. "You must be anvil or hammer," Goethe had once said.

They walked along that boulevard and stopped in front of the building housing the Imperial Museum. With its imposing façade and radiant luxuriousness, the emperor's summer palace resembled the Hotel Metropole in Vienna. The Metropole had since been taken over by the Gestapo. If the Germans ever reached Petrópolis, they would no doubt requisition this building too and turn it into their headquarters. They would love the rococo facade, the sumptuous rooms, its glitzy gilding, its majestic chandeliers. They loved everything that was flammable. He pictured the walls hung with giant portraits of Hitler instead of the emperor. The SS would have the time of their lives in the palace cellars, where they could revel in their games of torture.

Lotte felt tired. She was short of breath. Stefan uttered a few soothing words, they were almost there. Just a little farther, and they would be at the Hotel Solar do Império, where they had decided to lunch. A bellboy opened the door and welcomed them in English. Stefan was an Englishman here. They walked down a hall whose walls were studded with lively canvases depicting tropical landscapes. A waiter ushered them into the dining room. They took a seat next to the terrace, from where they could admire the boulders of the Serra dos Órgãos. Watching a mountain range in the middle of the jungle: the last show he'd ever see in his life. The pianist was playing a slow, melancholy *choro*. The waiters asked them what they would like to drink. Stefan ordered champagne and Lotte opted for *camarão casadinho*—shrimp served in puréed cassava—while Stefan dithered between duck with blackberry sauce and *bobó de camarão*. He asked for the waiter's recommendation. Each was excellent and they were completely different dishes, but which of these did he really fancy for lunch? Lotte decided for him, taking his hand in hers with an ironic smile on her lips. He said she was right to make fun of him. He couldn't even order lunch. He was going senile. She looked him in the eye and said, with a serious tone, her cheeks flushing a bright crimson as if she were about to do something terribly bold:

"You've never been able to make up your mind."

The champagne was poured. The music grew livelier. They drank, staring at one another intently in silence. When they'd drained their flutes, he wished her a happy anniversary. Tears streamed down Lotte's cheeks. She explained that she was overwhelmed.

"Two years of marriage…"

He got ready to propose a toast, to swear to her that they'd live to see their silver anniversary, but the waiter arrived with their first courses. He didn't want to make false promises.

They pictured themselves as they'd been two years earlier in Bath, where they'd snickered at the way the registrar had garbled Zweig's name twice. They'd had the annex of the council building all to themselves. They hadn't had any witnesses or friends. No white dress or bridal train for her. Nor a veil or a tiara. They had each said "yes" in their own way: Lotte had done so passionately, while Stefan had replied as though his answer were just a formality. After the registrar had pronounced them married, they had felt embarrassed. When the time had come to walk down the steps of the council building, he'd felt as though he'd just married his own daughter.

Two days later, they had received a missive from the council. Tearing the envelope open, thinking it was the mayor sending him his best wishes, he instead saw that it bore the letterhead of the Foreign Office, informing him that he had been designated an "enemy alien". The British declaration of war on the Reich had made him a potential enemy of the Crown. An attached letter informed him of his rights and responsibilities. Mr Stefan Zweig was to be confined to house arrest, and allowed to roam free within a five-mile radius of his home. Breaching those conditions would result in criminal charges. Each time he wanted to go abroad, he would need to ask permission. He was forbidden to pass political comments on the situation. He would have to register with the council in person once a week. "They forgot to tell me to wear a yellow star," he had reacted. Hitler's soldiers had threatened him with death, Goebbels had put him in Category 1 of "undesirable and pernicious" writers. The Foreign Office had labelled him a Class B "enemy alien". He had missed out on Class A, which would have meant imprisonment! In London, he was an enemy and a stranger. As the Germans had summed up, a *Juden*, so the author of *Mary Stuart* was an enemy of the British Crown? What were they afraid of? That Stefan Zweig would launch an attack on 10 Downing Street? Had Freud, his mentor and friend, received a similar letter from the Foreign Office before his death? Was Freud a Class B, an enemy alien? Freud had happily preferred to leave this world behind, in his own manner, at a time of his own choosing.

Vermin in Germany, they were now lepers in Great Britain.

He had moved to London in 1934, choosing the latter over Paris, whose political climate was too unstable thanks to its cabals and factions. He had gone to London to make a break with Austria. He had put down his suitcases believing it was as if he'd surrendered his weapons. He'd hoped the distance would put him beyond the reach of those demons. Yet the demons had followed him, crossing the Continent and the Channel, where they had started haunting the island. The Devil had taken up residence in his very soul.

He had put himself out of harm's way while they tortured his friends in Dachau. With each passing month, the Reich built another step for the gallows. When he'd first arrived in London, he'd lived in an apartment on Hallam Street. He had then moved to the smaller town of Bath, in the vicinity of Bristol. Following five long years of exile, he had obtained a passport thanks to the intervention of Bernard Shaw and H.G. Wells—and when he had finally become a British citizen, war had been declared on Germany. As a result, people started seeing spies around every street corner. It became inadvisable to be heard speaking German. Suspicion weighed heavily on the exiles. On that passport, which he'd won after a protracted struggle, they had added "enemy alien" in black ink. Enemy of the Reich and the British Crown. He had become a pariah. An ardent humanist, Zweig had become an enemy of the human race.

Since he preferred exile over dishonour, he had left London for New York. After that, he had also escaped from New York. Fleeing had been his way of living in the world. Salzburg London, London–New York, New York–Rio, and, after Rio, where next?

"There weren't only downsides to living in London," she smiled.

It was thanks to their London exile that they'd been able to meet. Stefan had settled there in the spring of 1934, whereas she had already been there for a year, having fled Katowice alongside her brother as soon as Hitler had come to power. In a worrying twist of irony, Friderike had introduced them to one another. His wife had insisted that Stefan hire a personal secretary to assist him during the writing of *Mary Stuart*, after having lost his former secretary, the loyal Anna Meingast. Lotte had kept silent throughout most of the interview. Had he been seduced by her shyness, the allure of her submissiveness and wide-eyed adoration, which Lotte hadn't been able to conceal? She had only been twenty-five years old, whereas he had been in his early fifties.

As soon they'd laid eyes on one another, Friderike had been under no illusions. Yet she hadn't become suspicious. Throughout the many years she'd lived with the writer, she'd seen a great number of mistresses come and go. She had resigned herself to being married to a philanderer. She only demanded a little discretion. She demanded silence. With Lotte, however, things had taken an unexpected turn.

The three of them had met the previous summer at the Hôtel Westminster along the Promenade des Anglais in Nice. Lotte had taken a room next to the married couple's. They had spent a month there during the summer of 1934 with Joseph Roth and Jules Romains. They had attended a concert given by their friend Toscanini at the Opéra de Monte-Carlo and taken long leisurely walks up and down the Grande Corniche. One morning in July, Friderike had gone to the consulate to see about her visa and had returned a little earlier than expected. Like a character in a bad play, she had surprised her husband and his secretary holding hands on the balcony.

A woman crossed the dining room of the Hotel Solar do Império with a spring in her step. Her hair was short and a little grizzled. She was wearing beige flannel trousers and a black shirt. Stefan could not avoid watching her silhouette glide between the tables.

"She bears a slight resemblance to Friderike," Lotte calmly commented.

He denied it.

"Yes, something about her presence. Your wife cut quite an appearance."

He retorted that *she* was now his wife.

"Do you miss her sometimes?"

He shook his head.

"I'm certain you miss her, or that you're going to miss her. Maybe we shouldn't have left New York."

He remembered the last time he'd seen Friderike, and strange as it might seem, that encounter had happened purely by chance. They had found themselves face to face in an office on Fifth Avenue, where both parties had come to fill in their visa applications. It had been months since they'd last seen one another. He had wanted to embrace her, but hadn't given in to his desire. He had cut the emotional outpourings short. He hated effusiveness. Was this chance encounter a sign? Were those implausible reunions just before their departure for Rio meant to make him give up his plans and stay in New York with Alma and Franz Werfel, with Thomas Mann and Jules Romains? To dwell among his people?

The waiter served the main course. They'd run out of duck with blackberry sauce and so the chef had made him a *bobó de camarão*. Stefan reacted indifferently. Lotte turned to the waiter and said:

"It's nothing serious you know, he's never been able to make up his mind."

He started reminiscing about the old days. He loved to tell stories about the early hours of the new century, when he'd been a twenty-year-old in Vienna. He knew that she'd always found his anecdotes entrancing. It seemed like time travel to her, allowing her to think she too had been twenty and by his side. Sometimes, when he wasn't in the mood, she would insist:

"Tell me one of your stories. I love it when you talk about yourself, you're such a good storyteller. I want to know everything about you. The present and the past. I want to have been a spectator to every second of your life. I want to be you, to stand by your side, I want to have been there, at the Café Beethoven, the Burgtheater, to stroll with you in the Volksgarten, to admire Maximiliansplatz, to mount the steps of the Opera next to you, to breathe the air of Marienbad. Destiny decided I was to be

41

born much too late, so I want to make up for lost time, I want to know all about those years when we were apart—tell me!"

He would begin to evoke the highlights of his life. The sound of waltzes would start to resound in Lotte's soul. Fans would start to flutter as young ladies with gloved hands and wonderful dresses leant on the arms of Imperial Army officers, dressed in their white uniforms, their chests studded with bright medals. Hearing his story, she would find herself arm in arm with him in the ballroom of the Hofburg Palace. The young couples in front of them swayed to the rhythm of the music. There were paintings by Klimt on the walls next to the portraits of the Emperor Franz Josef. Huge chandeliers burst into showers of light. She listened to him, dumbstruck, guided by his speech. They danced around his words. They relished being together, just the two of them. She heard a word slip past his lips which she'd never hitherto heard him say, and which he never said without feeling doubtful. He never said "I love you", never promised they'd spend their whole lives together, that their love was greater than all others before it; he had never expressed the wish that a child might spring forth from her loins, a son that would bear his name, Zweig, who would be the son of Stefan Zweig and Elizabeth Charlotte Altmann, grandson of Moriz and Ida Zweig and Arthur Salomon and Sarah Eva Altmann.

All of a sudden, it was as if night had fallen outside. A swarm of black and grey clouds obscured the sky. The horizon was striped with lightning. The thunder roared. After that, the rain fell in a great crash. He told her not to be afraid. She replied that she feared nothing so long as she was by his side.

She cared little about the rain and the thunder. Her womb was still sterile. She would never feel a baby's shrieking on her breast, she would never cradle him sweetly in her arms. The horizon faded into the earth. He picked up his story where he'd left off. She was no longer listening to him. Her mind was elsewhere. She thought about Eva on New York's streets. After a few minutes, the downpour came to an end. The waiter brought over the bill. Just as quickly as it had blackened, the sky was restored to an azure blue.

They left the palace. He hailed the man at his post in front of the hotel, who was holding the reins of a two-horse carriage. They started back.

OCTOBER

H E GOT OUT OF BED slowly and quietly, taking care not to
wake her. Once on his feet, he contemplated his features,
his wrinkle-free face, bright as an opal, his long eyelashes and his
wavy locks, which fell to the nape of his neck. Lotte was sleeping on
her side, her right arm folded towards the corner of a pillow, as if
she'd been looking for a shoulder to lie on. He admired her slender
wrist, adorned by a gold bracelet he'd given her the previous night.
Her body was only half-covered and her nightshirt allowed him
to glimpse a figure that hadn't lost any of its sensuality despite
all the privations of exile. Her chest rose at intervals that seemed
a little too close together, but her breathing was regular. For the
past two weeks she had slept soundly. Her illness was kept at bay.

That place was paradise. When he woke in the middle of
the night, he saw her fast asleep and breathing peacefully. The
asthma attacks were a distant memory now. This place brought
people back from the dead.

He felt safe. It was just a shame there were newspapers keeping
him in touch with developments around the world. There was
also the radio, and he understood Portuguese. Then there were
letters from fellow exiles, who, having just left Europe, had sent
him reports that prophesied a coming doomsday. Blood oozed
from their lips.

He left the room, shut the door behind him, crossed the corridor, walked right up to the veranda and, standing behind the window, gazed at the sweeping vista that stretched before him. The valley to the west was steeped in fog. A white-satin veil hung over the maize plantations, which were lit by a few reddish hearths. The city's houses were wrapped in a thick mist. He opened the window and filled his lungs with the sweetly scented air. The sun rose above the mountain. Everything turned crimson. Soon enough, his eyes could no longer bear the intensity of the light. He went back into the lounge and sat down in a rocking chair.

He hadn't slept a wink that night. Even less than usual. Sleep had already eluded him for a long time. He had left his dreams behind in Austria. At night, he met with his lost loved ones. All his dear departed reached out to him from the afterlife to pay him a visit. The guests queued at his door. They talked about the rain and fine weather, they shared their foolish hopes, broke down into tears and laughed heartily.

He preferred night to day, when he would hear the voices of his nearest and dearest, even when not in bed. Regardless, he would never again hear his mother's sweet tone, or Joseph Roth's complaints, or experience Rathenau's friendly smugness, Schnitzler's melancholic smile, Rilke's enthusiasm or Freud's stern looks. The faces of loved ones peered out of the penumbra of the night. They were timeless moments. Sadly, the first streaks of dawn scattered their images, snuffing out their murmurs and laughter, putting an end to the past, to people, to life. Everything reverted to stony silence. Preferring the company of ghosts, he began to be frightened by the living.

His lids never closed, his eyes stayed wide open. The sleepless nights unlocked inaccessible worlds, throwing open the doors of the past. He found himself walking backwards on a bridge suspended over a misty emptiness populated by familiar faces. He didn't regret his sleeplessness in the slightest. Nevertheless, his insomnia began to alter his perception of reality. He counted the moments until dusk. Ghosts invited themselves along even during the day while he was in the midst of the living. He had to restrain himself from greeting them. He was afraid people would think he'd lost his mind.

That night, Joseph Roth had dropped in for a chat. Roth had been his most assiduous visitor. A bold, wretched fighter, a pathetic and glorious warrior of words. Roth was the best man among them. Neither he, Thomas Mann nor Werfel would ever be capable of writing a single chapter that had both the power and the magnitude of *The Radetzky March*. He admired the writer, the fighter, the man who threw himself head first into every struggle. He envied Roth's despondency as much as his genius. Roth had lingered in Vienna until the last moment. Roth had fought, Roth wasn't a coward who had holed up in the mountains of Amazonia. Stefan had envied Roth's beginnings as well as his end. Roth had stood his ground alone, his body ravaged by absinthe, in the face of the proud, invincible soldiers pouring out of Germany. For months on end, Roth had staggered down the steps of his hotel on the Rue de Tournon, holding on to futile hopes fuelled by his drunkenness, declaring he was off to fight the armies of the Reich that were howling at France's door. A man with a thirst for divine grace and cheap wine had braved the tidal wave of organized savagery. In his newspaper columns, lectures and meetings with French politicians—and even Chancellor Schuschnigg himself—Roth had fought against the *Anschluss* right up to the moment when the Germans marched into Vienna. In the meanwhile, Stefan hadn't dared sign the slightest petition or pen the briefest article. He had been paralysed by the repercussions his words might incur.

Germans were plunging their spikes deep into the bellies of Jews and he hadn't dared to speak out lest it wound up being interpreted as a provocation. He had brought shame on himself. He had never stopped supporting Roth, had even invited the writer to join him in Britain and accompany him to the United States, and had sent him money orders every three months. Friderike had looked after him in Paris, helping him up the steps of the hotel on Rue de Tournon, propping up a man who was digging himself a grave with alcohol. One day, floored by the news of Ernst Toller's suicide in New York, Roth had died. The previous night, Friderike and Soma Morgenstern had had him moved to the Necker Hospital. On the other hand, Stefan hadn't even had the courage to come down from London to attend the funeral service.

Roth had reappeared that night. He had slid past the curtains and sat down next to the bed. He was holding a glass in his hand and was pouring himself large whiskies while his body trembled from tip to toe. On that night, the writer had come to enquire after his wife's health. Roth's wife, a schizophrenic, was also called Friederike.

"Is it true what the exiles are saying?" Roth had asked him.

Carried by a doom-laden voice that had risen out of the depths of the netherworld, Stefan had heard a rumour louder than all the war drums. He hadn't believed his ears. Could it be that such terror, suffering, savagery, hate and inhumanity had rained down on a single human being, especially one as innocent as Friederike Roth, one whose mind had been torn to shreds ever since she'd fallen prey to madness in 1929? Had the German monsters really done what people were accusing them of? Had they really euthanized poor Friederike? Roth's body shook with painful and protracted tremors.

"No, it's not true," Zweig had murmured, "you shouldn't

believe everything doomsayers tell you. They have a tendency to make horrors sound even more horrible. You know how Germans are, they are capable of the worst, but would they go to such extremes? What would they care about hunting down and overpowering such a lost, simple soul in the grips of madness? Germans extol the virtues of warriors, and celebrate the rights of the strong over the weak. Do you think that the Germans would detract their attention from the conquest of the world to chase after someone as poor and weak as Friederike Roth? Rest in peace, my dear Roth, in your world of tranquillity, goodness and solicitude, our promised land."

"You've put my mind at ease," Roth had whispered. "Is there any news of her then other than these abject lies?"

"My dear Joseph, have no fear, they were able to rescue your wife. She's doing well. She's in Switzerland, we helped her cross the border and she is safe from those demons coming out of Germany, as well as the ones haunting her soul. A psychiatrist is looking after her in a Geneva clinic."

"Good thing she's in Switzerland, she'll be all right. Blessed are the Swiss who take us in and dress our wounds. Do you know the doctor's name?"

"Yes, it's Alfred Döblin, our dear Alfred, that great physician, that renowned writer, the one who looked after her in Berlin and referred her to Dr Bernstein, a disciple of Freud, and who looks after those of us who've lost their minds down here."

"If he's a disciple of Freud, then she's saved."

Then they had talked about their work.

"One day," Roth's voice had said, "you're going to read my latest novella, you're going to like it, it's written in your style, and I think I'm going to call it *Job*. What about you? Are you writing? We must write, we must write books that are flame-proof."

He had replied that he was in the middle of finishing his autobiography.

"That's good," Roth had said approvingly, "tell your readers about what our world was once like, be a witness to your times, we must be witnesses. An autobiography, that's good."

"You're in the right place for that."

"You've always kept me in a special place in your heart. You've always been there for… I'm happy to go on my journey now that I know that my wife, my little lost one, is finally able to sleep in peace."

After that, dawn had arrived.

Now that he'd woken up, he pondered Friederike Roth's destiny. Married to Roth and a schizophrenic, she'd been hunted down by the Gestapo, who after looking for her in Berlin, had finally tracked her down in Munich, after someone blew the whistle on her. The exile community had related how the Gestapo had surprised her in a tiny deserted flat, huddled up, having lost all faculties of speech, in a room plunged in darkness. The SS had grabbed her by the wrists and, since she'd clung to herself tightly, emitting long frightened, demented cries, they had pistol-whipped her and dragged her broken body out while a faint breath of life still coursed through it. They had led her to a truck where they'd kept other madmen, some of whom were howling, while others were immured behind a wall of silence. The truck had driven into the middle of the woods, right up to a magnificent building on the outskirts of Linz, the psychiatric hospital of Linz, an establishment that had been renowned in the late 1920s. Mrs Roth had woken up in a room filled with dozens of other mentally ill patients. In the midst of terrified cries, they had come to collect her, as well as other tortured souls. They had led Mrs Roth into a bare room and under the Nazi policy "Aktion T4", which aimed to eliminate patients suffering with mental illnesses, they had administered an injection of strychnine. Friederike Roth had been murdered.

Zweig rose and gave one last thought to his friend. At least he'd been spared all of this.

They had purchased tickets for Rio. The train would leave Petrópolis at ten o'clock. They would reach Rio in time for lunch. They waited on the small station's deserted platform. Stefan was wearing his beige suit, while Lotte wore a pale-blue cotton dress. He was carrying a bulky folder under his arm. He looked worriedly around him.

"No one's going to steal anything from you, you know," she said mockingly.

Her comment cheered him up for a few seconds, then he reverted to a sombre disposition. Two adolescents were crossing the platform just a few metres ahead of him. He took three steps back and clenched the folder tightly.

"You're not running any risks. Who's going to steal a manuscript? People barely have enough to eat."

It was a joke, but she knew how important the manuscript was to him. She understood his fear of losing it. In a way, it was as if he were holding his life in his hands. The book spoke of a world that didn't exist any more outside the memories of a few people. That world had been annihilated. Who else would have been able to tell the story of that defunct era? Who would have the genius to bring its splendour back to life? He was the last, the only one who could pass this light on to future generations. This book was almost a relic.

She was intimately acquainted with each and every sentence. Some phrases had been etched into her soul: "So I ask my memories to speak and choose for me, and give at least some faint reflection of my life before it sinks into the dark." She had read all his books. He had never before written anything as beautiful and profound, or as silvery and sad.

She was the one who had typed up each page on her old Remington. She had typed out the title, *The World of Yesterday*. He was still dithering over the title. He thought about calling it *Lost Generation, Memoirs of a European* or *My Three Lives*. They had worked for six months on that book. She thought "they" because, yes, she'd had a role in its shaping. Stefan would draft it in his notebooks, whose loose leaves she would then type up. He would reread the pages, make his corrections and scrawl endless additions in the margins. She would then retype the corrected text.

She said: "It's good as it is, it's perfect, there's nothing left to change, it's your best book yet."

He went back to work, spent whole days and nights correcting the text. He worked tirelessly and never seemed satisfied after reading each version. No, he would explain, that isn't worthy of what I experienced. The trick is to describe both the light and the shadows, war and peace, the grandeur and the decadence. He wrecked his health writing that book, and slightly lost his mind over it too.

He had begun work on his memoirs in New York, but had felt incapable of remembering each episode of his life and then piecing them together like a jigsaw puzzle. He'd usually had a number of notes at his disposal and worked in libraries. But he had nothing that might help jog his memory. He had then thought of seeing Friderike again. Worse still, he had chosen to up sticks and leave town so as to rekindle his relationship with his ex-wife. Stefan and Lotte had left New York and relocated to a sad, dingy hotel in the

town of Ossining, for the sole reason that Friderike lived in the
vicinity. Stefan would leave their hotel room each morning and
go to meet his ex-wife. He excused himself by blaming his failing
memory. He was forced to draw from the well of his ex-wife's
memories. He would leave in the morning and come back in the
evening. Nothing carnal went on between them, Lotte knew that.
It was even worse than that. Picturing him by her side as they
walked hand in hand down the road of their radiant past was more
terrible than the thought of them sharing a bed. The following day
she'd worn her eyes out staring at her Remington and experienced
the same dread as if she'd witnessed them embracing. Friderike
knew everything, remembered everything. There had only ever been one
Mrs Zweig and this book would stand as a testament to that until
the end of time. Lotte didn't belong to the world of yesterday. That
book was her coffin, and she'd even nailed the planks together.
Stefan and Friderike had known each other for thirty years—by
contrast, what did the few years he and Lotte had spent together
really amount to? Friderike von Winternitz had witnessed all of
his moments of glory, his triumphs, the rapturous welcomes he'd
received in Berlin, Paris and Rome. Friderike was the one who'd
known the gates of Viennese palaces, the staircases adorned with
flowers, the sound of violins, of orchestras, valets in their red
livery, the dresses cut of pink tulle, the flamboyant hairstyles, the
lacy shawls, the velour ribbons, wrists weighed down by bracclcts,
the opening bars of music and the intoxicating dances, fine pearls
hung round necks, the sophisticated dishes that were served,
boudoirs where suitors whispered words of love while mazurkas
played in the background, small salons and great excitement,
palaces in Switzerland and trips in first class, private theatre boxes
that were both peaceful and curtained off by dusky red curtains,
the hours of great successes, the immortal moment of the initial

thrills, the magic cast by the first laurels. Friderike was the one who'd savoured the honours, the sweet words of praise, seen the future throw open its doors, the marble palaces, the proud palominos galloping through the cool evening breeze. Lotte instead had been dealt the bottomless pits of despair, the terror-stricken visions, the path of exile, third-class compartments, the shabby bungalows and the rattling carriages pulled by donkeys. She had teetered between indifference on the one hand and despair on the other. The worst had been saved for last: five years after Stefan and Friderike had divorced, here he was running after her again. Reliving what they'd already experienced.

Would that one of those adolescents stole that manuscript of his! Lotte's name hadn't appeared even once throughout the book's four hundred pages. There had only been a single entry in his journal:

Wednesday, 6th September 1939: We had a quick breakfast, I shaved, then came the wedding, officiated with least amount of fuss, only a simple vow: I hereby take L.A. as my lawful wedded wife.

Thursday, 7th September: A whole host of small affairs to put in order.

She stared at him as he clutched the manuscript to his chest. He was still holding Friderike in his arms. A metallic rattle on the other side of the platform. A whistle blow resounded. A swirl of black smoke. The train came to a stop. They climbed into the second carriage. She sat down in front of him and saw him cast his gaze about, no doubt to reassure himself that the adolescents hadn't followed him. The train left the platform. He placed the precious package on his knees, then he held his hand out to his wife. His grip effaced the memory of Friderike Maria von Winternitz.

53

She stood up and went to stand by the window. The suburbs of the Imperial City had a desolate splendour to them thanks to those large mansions, which were utterly deserted at this time of year. Farther on, they passed by a few villas overrun by tropical vegetation, then some huts where half-naked children were busy playing. They entered a forest. Lotte shut her eyes and took a deep breath of the air coming in through the window. It was impregnated with the perfume of bananas, mangoes and rosebay. She opened her eyes on a vast plain, in the middle of which was a lake bathed in light. They pressed on, cradled by the hacking cough of the machines. A ruined church rose above the rugged boulders. The train descended into a valley. Struck by vertigo, Lotte sat back down.

He hadn't even flinched. His face, as well as his body, seemed frozen exactly as it had been when she had left him a few moments earlier. His eyes were fixed on the compartment door, while his hands were still holding the folder on top of his knees. Slowly, his head began to nod and his eyelids started to shut. His parted lips partially revealed a toothless mouth. All that travelling had ravaged his teeth. That was the other reason for their trip to Rio. The man who had once been a Viennese dandy would soon be fitted with a steel jaw. He hadn't wanted her to accompany him to the dentist's. He had said he didn't need her to hold his hand when the drill sank into his jaw. He still had his pride after all, despite being an old man. "You're not even sixty yet," she had retorted. "I'll come! I've followed you to the ends of the earth, I might as well go with you to the dentist's." He had given in in the end. She had whispered in his ear:

"I would follow you to the depths of hell."

The movement of the train tipped his head against the window. Lotte was scared that the contact with the glass might wake him up. She took off her jacket, folded it and slid it against his cheek. She examined his face. No, he hadn't aged. He still looked impeccably stylish and effortlessly aristocratic. His hair was like that of a forty-year-old. His brown moustache gave his face a flirtatious edge, adding to his natural elegance. She wondered how he must have looked aged twenty. She'd never paid attention to young men. She'd only ever liked mature men. Truth be told, she hadn't ever loved anyone except him. There he was now, sleeping like a baby. She would never have children. He felt too old to become a father. He also refused to bring a new life into this hostile world. His other wife hadn't cared much about that as she'd already had two daughters from a previous marriage.

Lotte had resigned herself in the end. Would her health have allowed her to become a mother? "You'll die in childbirth," the doctors had warned. She didn't want to die in childbirth. She didn't want to die at all. That's why she had followed him, all the way to the end of the world. So he could protect her. He gave her the feeling he knew where he was going. He had the gift of seeing into the future. He'd known when to leave Austria and when to leave England. He was equipped with a sixth sense, he knew the bleak horizons towards which the world was headed. He knew how to decide where they should run away to.

He opened his eyelids and suddenly straightened himself up. He asked her whether he'd dozed off. He sounded irked. She told him he hadn't. Stefan leant towards her, looked her right in the eye and told her they would be happy here. But he kept pursing his lips. Those words were devoid of any real joy, lightness or reassurance. He wanted to dispel the effect his words had left behind, whereupon she felt the incandescent warmth of his fingers in the hollow of her hand. He asked her if she doubted him. Did she think he was lying to her?

"I believe you," she said, "I will always believe you."

"Good," he said. He wanted her to forgive his mood swings and bouts of melancholy. He hadn't been able to repress the feelings of horror that continually assailed him.

"I know," she murmured.

From time to time, his soul seemed impenetrable to the light. Everything was pervaded by shadows and suffering. He found himself in a dark wood whose trees had turned into bodies.

"You're not walking alone any more, I'm right here beside you in the middle of that forest and I'm holding your hand."

She had to forgive him. Some days, everything exuded a heavy weariness as life woke up in the middle of a vanished past. Could she understand that? There was nothing she couldn't understand. He was deaf to the sound of mellow birdsong, the promise of a coming springtime, or even the heralding of a new day. The spark of life was missing. Time stood still, the stream of hours and minutes had come to a halt on that morning of 6th March 1934 when he'd left Austria. The giant clock of Vienna's railway station had come to a stop. Time had frozen. He felt as if he'd been cast off to the other side of the world. She understood that, didn't she? He had been given everything only for it to have been taken away. Needless to say, he didn't have the right to wallow in that state of mind, or feel sorry for himself. He was privileged. Most of his friends didn't have imaginary demons snapping at their heels. Their demons were very real, and those demons had sworn to vanquish them as well as all their nearest and dearest. He didn't have the right to throw in the towel.

"Of course you have the right to," she said, "you don't have a warrior's insensitivity. You feel things more deeply. You're a writer."

He knew he had to look strong in front of the legions of the weak-willed, but his strength abandoned him. He was being seduced by the void.

"You only need to rest, to relax a little. You're going to recover your health here."

He forced a faint smile.

"Look over there, look outside," she exclaimed.

It was the most breathtaking panorama. The horizon opened up. Earth, water and fire filled an immensity of space. The sky stretched into a gigantic arc. Bright-green ranges of hills sloped down to valleys seemingly teeming with life. The jungle wrapped its tentacles around little white houses. Nestled under the shade of palm trees, an agglomeration of huts was wedged in between various paths. All of a sudden, Rio came into view: a horde of skyscrapers perched in the middle of a row of palaces and avant-garde architecture. The city was enveloped by the foamy arm of the ocean, dotted by green islets, ocean liners and sailing boats. To the right was *Christ the Redeemer* atop Corcovado, which stood guard over that world of giants. Everything was limitless and illuminated. The more the train forged ahead, the more the contours of the world seemed to widen. Beauty had been bequeathed to each corner of the world, and far from being overwhelmed by such magnificence, man in his haughtiness thrived in it.

He broke the silence. Sounding gloomy, he asked her if she thought the tooth pulling was going to hurt.

She didn't reply.

They hailed the first taxi in front of the station and climbed in. Lotte gave the driver the name of the hotel where they were expected.

"The Copacabana?" the taxi driver said. "That's the prettiest place in the world!"

They cut through alleyways, then took to a highway ruled by a state of constant restlessness. "You'd think we were in New York!" Lotte exclaimed. She rolled the window down. He cried out, telling her to be careful since the air simply had to be saturated with dust and dirt.

"I'm afraid of nothing here!" she exclaimed.

He envied her high spirits and thought that she was right, one had to live day by day and dispel the belief that tomorrow would be worse than yesterday. To recognize the fact that they were safe. Nobody would come looking for them here. The taxi crawled along a street lined with shops and luxury hotels. His eyes fell on a sign bearing the name Alberto Stern. He couldn't spot any notices calling for murder on the window, nor any saying "*Juden*" or "*Raus!*". There was no poster denouncing a Jewish conspiracy on the walls, no caricatures of pot-bellied, hook-nosed bankers with pockets bursting full of money.

"Where are you from?" the taxi driver asked.

Lotte replied that they'd arrived the previous month on a ship from the United States.

"Are you Americans?"

"No."

"You don't look like you are. We love all strangers here, except for Americans. The Americans think they're at home everywhere they go… You're Europeans, that much is clear, you're clearly people of fine taste. We love elegance, don't let the dirty streets fool you. Brazilians are a great people… And you, which tribe do you belong to? You have a German accent. We've had plenty of Germans here in the past few years. Those Germans are really nice. They fit in quickly. They were paupers when they first arrived, but within the space of ten years they've bought up half of Rio. So much the better, it'll be good for business. I believe in the economy. Whole boatfuls of Germans come ashore every day. I'm all for it. I go to the docks every day at eight o'clock on the dot and wait. A single family will earn my keep for the day. Although, between you and me, they're not as generous as they used to be. One might say the good times have come to an end. Boats and people's pockets don't seem as full as they used to be. So, are you Germans?... Austrians maybe? That's also good... One of my customers told me that Austria didn't exist any more, that it had become just another German province. I'm not into politics. The Germans wanted Hitler, nobody forced them. Brazil might also benefit by being ruled by someone with an iron fist. President Vargas is the right man for the job. Vargas will never let the communists get to Rio. We have a saying here, 'We've got room for Jews, but not for communists.' Are you communists? Whether you're Jewish or not doesn't bother me. Look at our Redeemer up on that hill over there, he belonged to the tribe of Israel. He watches over us. In any case, we've got room for all the world's poor; and from what I've been hearing on the news, it sounds like the world's poor are mostly Jews at the moment. Between you and me—and I say this because you don't strike me as Jewish—what goes around, comes around! Before all this, the Jews had all the wealth in the world. The tables have turned. When all is said and done, they'll come out the other side one day. They've honed their survival instincts. The only problem is that there's so many of them here now, and they occupy such positions of influence, that thanks to the grudge they've got against Hitler, they might very well drag us into the war. Look at what they're doing in America—they're always knocking on Roosevelt's door and they'll wind up winning the American people over to their cause, even though Americans are pacifists. Pacifists to a fault I should add. Look where the French wound up thanks to Blum.

Those German bastards marched right through the Arc de Triomphe! Blum clearly couldn't stand a chance against Hitler. Jews are good at business and making fine speeches, but put a gun in their hands and they're clueless. Have you seen the newsreels of German troops in Paris? Without taking sides, I must admit they looked rather great, and, after all, the French might benefit from being taken down a peg or two. So long as those Yids don't drag us into the war—otherwise I won't see them as friends any more. Hitler's done nothing to me, quite the opposite in fact, he's been good for business. The war's got nothing to do with us. Let the Jews go and fight if they want to, the boats are waiting in the docks, ready to sail for Germany. They can stay provided they only want to swim in the bay. There's no such thing as racism here in Rio. We've already got Indians, so we can cope with the Jews. All they need to understand is that each has to keep to his own, look at the Indians, they stay put in the *favelas*, you'll never see one of them at the Hotel Copacabana. Well, there we have it. You know, my job would be a lot less cheerful if I didn't have people like you to talk to."

The driver stopped the car in front of the hotel entrance, asked for his fare, got out and went to open Lotte's door, wished them a happy stay and bid them goodbye. They lingered in a sort of daze in front of the hotel's marquee, standing still as a warm wind blew in from the sea. Their eyes followed the taxi as it drove back into the fray. They exchanged a silent look, feeling stunned and outraged. They stepped into the hotel, walking slowly, their arms linked, looking as uncertain and awkward as if they'd just walked away from a road accident, unscathed but groggy. They crossed the grand lobby, whose walls were decorated with reproductions of Otto Kirchner's portraits. There were a few men in suits working their way through a bottle while sitting on white leather sofas.

Their voices blended into an indiscernible tangle. Stefan and Lotte gave their names at reception and asked for Abrahão Koogan, the man they were due to meet. An employee pointed them in the direction of the terrace, where Koogan was expecting them.

They had barely set foot outside when they felt as though they'd been blinded by the light, a burning brightness that flooded over everything and seemed to rise out of the ocean and solidify in the atmosphere. Warm voices and hearty laughter resounded under the taut white canvas awnings, which were being gently stirred by the wind. It was like standing on the deck of a sailing boat. Abrahão Koogan, the Brazilian publisher, was sitting alone at a table, dressed in white, with a Super Fino Montecristi on his head. Koogan got up and greeted them effusively. They embraced warmly.

Koogan expressed his joy at seeing them again. A whole year had gone by, yes, it was in fact a full year since they'd last met, in September 1940. He recalled episodes from Zweig's South American lecture tour—he called it a triumph, how else could one describe those crowds who had come to listen to the author whose books had then sold by the thousands? Koogan listed the countries they'd visited. No one else could achieve that kind of success. No other author in the world. Not even Thomas Mann. Koogan stressed how proud he was to be Zweig's editor, the editor of the greatest living writer of their time.

"Would you like some champagne to celebrate our reunion?"

Stefan declined Koogan's offer. "The greatest living writer of their time," Koogan repeated. Stefan was very fond of Abrahão Koogan and therefore forgave him his excessive excitability. Koogan spoke of a time that no longer existed. His books had been banned all over Europe. He no longer had a homeland, or even a house.

"Is it true that you're learning Portuguese?" Koogan enquired.

Stefan replied in the affirmative. He was fluent in French and English. During his South American tour, he had given his lectures in Spanish. He entertained the slightly foolish notion that he would one day have learnt so many languages that his German vocabulary would simply dissolve into the melting pot of foreign words. The German language would be nothing but a dead tongue in his mouth. He would expel it with a cough. Then and only then would he be able to get on with his life. Nevertheless, German was a stubborn tongue. Even though it had poisoned the universe, its honeyed words still flowed effortlessly from his mouth.

"Reveal all," Koogan said, "I'm eager to hear what's in that manuscript you've brought along with you."

Zweig held out the package, asking him to take care of it. He only had two copies, and the second copy had left Rio the previous night and was headed for Sweden, being intended for that dear Gottfried Bermann-Fischer, who was currently living in exile in Stockholm and who had set up a small German-language imprint there. When he'd dropped the package off at the post office, he'd felt as though he were throwing a message in a bottle out to sea. By the time the ship reached its destination, the Germans would undoubtedly have conquered Sweden.

"I'm extremely proud to be the first to hold one of your books," Koogan said excitedly, "and it doesn't matter which book it is. Your autobiography!" He lifted his eyes to the heavens. "I'm holding *The World of Yesterday* in my hands!"

Who could still be interested in the story of his life? What had been the point of all those months he'd spent in America, sequestered in the prison of his past? He reproached himself for being so proud. For wanting to write a memoir while the fates of his nearest and dearest hung in the balance! Half of his friends were in cemeteries, while the other half were pacing around a German dungeon. He'd often felt ashamed of this project. In an attempt to exculpate himself, he'd tried to explain his motives for doing so. Strictly speaking, it wasn't really an autobiography. He hadn't wanted to tell the story of his life. It wasn't about him. His life wouldn't interest anyone. He could sum it up in a few words. He was born. He had written, he had never stopped writing. He had fled, he would never stop fleeing. He hadn't wanted to pour his heart out. The book's aim had been to describe the exceptional people he'd rubbed shoulders with. To paint a picture of an era that was on its way out, a world that the Nazis were desperately trying to obliterate. Writing that book had been like forging a funerary urn to accommodate all of those friends who hadn't received a proper burial. He had wanted to bear witness. He had wanted to erect a memorial stone in the midst of all those ruins. He had the terrible feeling that the swastika would fly from flagpoles in Berlin, Vienna—and the whole of Europe—for decades to come. He had resigned himself to no longer having a homeland. But he wanted to tell his readers that the world hadn't always been like this. He didn't know whether his book conveyed a hopeful message, or whether his readers would instead be plunged into deep despair. He'd never written any of his books with a message in mind. He had often been criticized for this. He wasn't *engagé*. He had nothing to say to the world other than recounting the wild passions experienced by his heroes and hero-ines. He envied the Manns—Thomas, Heinrich and Klaus—his namesake Arnold Zweig, that die-hard socialist. He also envied Martin Buber, Sholem Asch and Einstein, who had fought for the establishment of a Jewish state in Palestine. He didn't have any fixed ideologies. He hated ideologies. He had simply looked for the words to express "we existed". He wasn't sure he'd been able to bring the civilization he'd known to life in his books. You had to have grown up in Vienna in order to understand the scale of the atrocities it had suffered. He had wanted to engrave a message on a headstone that would prove to future generations that although it was now extinct, the world had once been home to a race called *Homo austrico-judaicus*. Those who read *The World of Yesterday* would not come across any revelations regarding how his mother had begrudged him her love, or how affectionate his father had been to his two sons. He hadn't written a word about his love life or his two wives. On perusing it, his readers might very well wonder whether he was all head and no heart. In fact, Stefan only appeared in the book as an observer. He had written it quickly, producing the first draft of four hundred pages in only six weeks. The man who had usually struggled to finish sixty-page novellas had penned four hundred pages in a month and a half. The only question left was what to call it. He had given up on *My Three Lives* for the reasons listed above, while *Our Generation* had struck him as too personal. He wasn't entirely satisfied with *The World of Yesterday*. Why not *Memoirs of a European*?

"You'll have all the time you need to settle on one," Koogan replied.

He kept quiet. Did he really have all the time to decide? He would turn sixty the following month. He'd lived long enough. He believed he'd seen enough.

Koogan pulled a cigar case out of his jacket's inside pocket and extracted a Virginia Brissago. He said:

"I believe they're your favourites."

Stefan explained he would smoke his later as he had to rush off to another important appointment. He added that Lotte and Koogan should remain seated and enjoy the sublime setting.

He wouldn't be long. Koogan consented cheerfully. Lotte gazed wistfully at her husband, wanting to remind him of her offer, but she refrained from doing so, pretending to acquiesce, but then added in a whisper:

"Are you sure you won't need me?"

But he'd already got up. He shook Koogan's hand and left.

NOVEMBER

E VERY MORNING he gazed at the heights of Petrópolis from the veranda, feasting his eyes, long since accustomed to drabness, on the splendour of the world. At dawn, he had an appointment with the light. The air filled with birdsong and the earth sprang back to life. Sometimes, he would catch himself thinking: today, the wind will bring gloomy clouds, black dust will obscure the sun and hummingbirds will launch into a death fugue. But no, each time the dawn illuminated the horizon. Life continued to unfurl like a wave.

He left his post to consume the breakfast the housekeeper had prepared for him. He drank his *cafezinho*, whose strong, sweet taste erased all trace of the aromas of the coffees he'd enjoyed in Michaelerplatz. Afterwards he sipped a glass of guava juice, sucked on a *jabuticaba* and savoured an *açaí* berry—which according to Rosaria was said to contain the elixir of youth.

Yet he couldn't stop himself from listening to the news. Japan was preparing to declare war on America. Admiral Dönitz's U-boats had unleashed a reign of terror on the oceans. German troops were advancing on the Soviet Union in the *Drang nach Osten*, or the push towards the east, the same policy that Ludendorff had employed in 1918, but which was now being implemented far more efficiently. Lithuania, Ukraine and the Crimea had fallen,

Kiev, Minsk, Leningrad and Riga had fallen—how could he not ponder the fates of those millions of Jews in their ghettos who were at the mercy of those Nazi soldiers? Goering's tanks were at the gates of Moscow and Operation Barbarossa had been an unqualified success. The Nazis were looting the world of its gold and leaving ashes and cinders in their wake.

The Germans had redefined the concept of evil. There were stories of soldiers going after children. As the Reich's armies advanced, they left small detachments of the SS behind, whose sole aim was to eliminate all Jews from conquered lands. The troops liquidated the ghettos. Soldiers fired their bullets into the skulls of mothers and their children, as well as all men, young and old alike. How far would they go? In the beginning, he had doubted these accounts. Besides, those reports sounded so similar he'd begun to question their veracity. Maybe he was the one who was losing his mind, having removed himself from the world. Horror had become the overriding truth of these times.

The following thought had impressed itself upon him: that news of barbarism's sweeping victories no longer affected him like it used to. He was able to redirect his gaze away from headlines bearing tales of catastrophes. Had he grown jaded? Was the warm breeze making his head spin? Did the *cachaça* that Rosaria served him—which she assured him had nothing but sugar cane in it—contain an evil potion? He liked to think that those little bitter-tasting red berries, which he relished despite not knowing what they were, had cast some sort of spell on him; or that the cult to which Rosaria belonged, in which she made offerings to idols and prayed to them, had produced its desired results. He thought about Exu, one of the earth deities Rosaria worshipped. Exu was a demigod whom he dreamt of imitating, a being who had neither friends nor enemies and who saw beyond good and evil—even though some people considered him the Devil incarnate.

A line by Heinrich Heine, the great Heine, whose books were also being burnt, kept coming back to him:

> When I think of Germany at night,
> It puts all thought of sleep to flight.

He didn't want to think about Germany. He hoped he might one day enjoy a full night's sleep.

The political situation in Rio was improving. Needless to say, the regime remained a kind of dictatorship, since Vargas had more in common with Franco than with Roosevelt. His Estado Novo had banned all political parties and thrown communists into prison. Still, even though the president, a follower of Machiavelli, had once made friendly overtures to the Reich, he was now realigning himself with the United States. Brazil's economic interests lay north, not east. The South allied to the North. All of America, the largest of the continents, was going to war with the Nazified Old World. No, the future didn't look too bleak.

He dared to hope again. A small miracle had occurred during the previous week. He had gone down into the cellar and had found a wooden case full of books amidst the jumble of furniture and linens. In it, there were three schoolbooks, two mathematics textbooks, a French dictionary and a number of Portuguese volumes. When he came across *The Kreutzer Sonata* and *Anna Karenina*, he saw himself back in 1928, in a thick wood alongside Tolstoy's daughter as they walked towards the genius's grave.

Then the miracle occurred. His hand had pulled out two volumes of Montaigne's *Essays*. The covers were graced with a portrait of Montaigne, who seemed to be smiling at him. He'd bundled the books under his arm and leapt up the stairs. Settling on the veranda, he'd begun to read, as though he'd just received a long-awaited letter from a distant friend. He had read the *Essays* as a young man, but what could stoicism, wisdom and self-control possibly have mattered to a twenty-year-old? He had been obsessed with Nietzsche at the time. He'd written an entire biography of Nietzsche, the very same Nietzsche whom Goebbels later adopted as his moral authority.

Times had changed. The world had begun to resemble the one that Montaigne had lived in. The earth was an inferno, an endless St Bartholomew's Day Massacre. His own life seemed to be taking the same course as the Frenchman's: the life of a recluse, a fugitive. The plague had descended over Europe, like it had once ravaged the kingdom of France. The plague had broken out in Montaigne's house, just like it had come knocking on his door at Kapuzinerberg. Stefan had fled Salzburg, just like Montaigne had quit his castle in Bordeaux. The Frenchman—a great-grandson of Moshe Paçagon—had wandered from town to town, an outcast, misunderstood, claiming to be afraid of dying, afraid of the plague, shouting that he wanted to live, to save his skin. Stefan and Montaigne weren't heroes. They had lived four hundred years apart, but had been driven by the same obsession: to remain true to themselves—during the St Bartholomew's Day Massacre and the Kristallnacht.

He read with great zeal. It was as if he were hearing a brother's voice whisper in his ear: "Don't worry about humanity as it self-destructs, go ahead and build your own world." It was a soothing voice imbued with wisdom and kindness. Having finished reading the first volume, he was seized by an idea. Since he wasn't able to finish his *Balzac*—he had neither the energy nor the talent to write about Balzac—why not write a biography of Montaigne? That would give him a reason to get out of bed each morning and go meet the brother whom destiny had sent his way—Stefan's actual brother, Alfred, had found asylum in New York, but despite the love he bore for him, they felt like strangers to one another. Indeed, what he shared with Montaigne was a brotherhood forged by destiny, and in order to write his biographies, he needed to feel impassioned by his subject matter, as well as to identify with it. "You're wonderfully versed in the art of transference," Freud had said. Talking about someone else was a way of talking about himself. He had written twenty or so essays, but he didn't think of himself as a historian, nor did he claim to be a biographer. He was a writer, that was all. The veracity of events was of secondary importance, and he was never worried about the business of working on the book itself. Jules Romains had been right to mock him for his inability to distance himself from his subjects, criticizing the confessional undertones coursing through his biographies, the inaccuracies that his writing was riddled with—ah, his *Stendhal*! He was only interested in individuals, in getting inside their minds, revealing their secrets and—rather than taking the stance of an erudite scholar—diving into the innermost depths of their souls, shedding light on those mysterious men and women. Yes, he was going to start work on *Montaigne*. Maybe writing it would allow him to learn how his subject had been able to hold on to his sanity? Writing about Montaigne might help him understand how he'd kept his humanity intact in the midst of all that barbarism.

*

Lotte woke up bright and early that morning. It had been a month since she'd recovered her health. Her asthma didn't disrupt her sleep any more and her heart rate had adopted a slower rhythm. She was once more the young woman he'd laid eyes on seven years earlier. The whole house was under a spell. The illness had been scared off. The Devil no longer darkened their door.

It was sometime around noon when Lotte came home. She had accompanied Rosaria to the market. They had walked along the Rua da Imperatriz and stopped in front of the cathedral, which was swarming with a crowd of worshippers; they had then gone down Avenida Koeler, admired the Palacio Rio Negro and crossed the canal to reach Praça Rui Barbosa.

"Rosaria thinks my accent has improved, and to think of all the trouble I had with English!... We stopped by a stall close to the Casa do Barão—the guava juice was delicious!"

Her voice no longer quivered. Her face no longer bore the signs of fear. Her melancholy had lifted entirely. She had come back to life.

"Today," she carried on, "Rosaria taught me a number of things. Soon I'll have learnt as much Portuguese as you and I'll finally be able to go to Rio on my own, seeing as how you don't enjoy going there and would prefer to stay here, which I can of course understand, you have to write, and you can finally get to down to work in total tranquillity. I would really love to stroll down the Avenida Rio Branco, go to the Praça Floriano theatre, walk on the beach... To ask 'Where is the bus stop?' you say: '*Onde é o ponto de ônibus?*'; 'a ticket for' is '*uma passagem para*'; 'I want to go' is '*Quero ir para*'; 'to go shopping' is '*fazer compras*', 'it's too expensive' is '*muito caro*'."

She burst out laughing.

"I want that dress: *muito caro!*"

He told her she could go to Rio by herself; they would book her a taxi and Koogan's nephews could take her around the city.

LAURENT SEKSIK

"What about you?" she asked. "You're the one I want by my side. I know it's not a good time for you. You've finally started writing again. I shouldn't distract you. Did you work well last night?"

He nodded. He had gradually recovered his focus. He had begun researching Montaigne at the public library in Petrópolis and, much to his surprise, had found quite a few books on the French writer on its shelves. Fate had given him another push in the right direction: Fortunat Strowski, the renowned authority on Montaigne, was now living in Rio. Koogan had offered to arrange a meeting.

"You see," she said, "the tide is turning. The bad times are already behind us."

She was right. The best was yet to come.

"It's such a beautiful day outside. Come and take the air with me, you'll go back to writing later feeling invigorated."

They went to a little square by Avenida Koeler and sat down on the terrace of a café, where a number of wealthy *cariocas* were also seated, no doubt enjoying their summer holiday in the resort.

They ordered. Soon enough, one of the ladies left her group, walked in their direction, stood in front of Stefan and launched into the following in a heavily accented English:

"Excuse me, you're... Stefan Zweig, aren't you? The newspapers have reported your presence in Petrópolis. My name is Consuela Burgos, my husband is Professor Burgos, the best surgeon in Rio... I've read all your books: *Beware of Pity*, *Fear* and *Downfall of the Heart*, and the one I've been rereading non-stop, *Twenty-Four Hours in the Life of a Woman*. I have always asked myself how a man could possibly penetrate the female psyche to such an extent. What's your secret, does it come down to research, do you interview women? Where do you dig up all of these truths? I tend to use an expression whenever I speak about you, I call you a soul searcher... Through you, I was able to visit Monte Carlo with Mrs C., the heroine of your book, and I must admit that I too fell madly in love with that young man and his beautiful hands... and, if I may confide in you, since you've become something of a friend, a friend whose words warm the heart, that I too once experienced such passions, unfortunately the affair was short-lived, but he stole my heart regardless, one should never trust men... Well, let's forget about the past. I have another confession to make: I have written some novellas, a little like yours, in which I describe women who have been ravaged by their passions, but my heroines are different from yours, they never think of putting their lives to an end, no, they're too keen on living for that, and don't you think that in a way they're right? Isn't life worth living in a place like this, which has been blessed by the gods? No, these ladies always wind up going back to their cherished husbands, who forgive their wives for having strayed, after all, it's only an affair. If you would be so kind, I will leave my manuscripts at the bar tomorrow and you'll get back to me about them, won't you? Don't make me wait too long, my calm appearance belies a tormented soul... Before I take my leave, I would like to thank you on behalf of the Brazilian people for your book *Brazil, Land of the Future*. My husband said that it was as if you'd anatomized our continent... But above all else, don't you listen to any of those criticisms launched against you, we know that this book wasn't commissioned by the government, that our president didn't pay you to sing this country's praises. You're an honest man, Mr Zweig, and even if your book regrettably paints a folkloristic portrait of Brazil, let me ask you, what else could one expect from a foreigner? And as I've said to those who criticized you: you specialize in the hearts of women, not the hearts of countries. It's as if someone asked my husband to treat tuberculosis, why he would just go ahead and remove the patient's lungs… You described Brazil exactly as you saw it, and as I'm standing right in front of you, I can confirm that your gaze is far more intense than photographs of you would suggest. You have an honest look in your eyes, and if your wife would allow me, because presumably this is your wife, delighted to meet you, madam, it's an honour, I expect you are fully aware of how privileged you are to be married to such a man, married to a man who probes the hearts of women, you better believe it, married to the man who pierces through men's bodies, you're really lucky… I don't want to take up too much of your time, so, before taking my leave, could you sign my handkerchief, there you are, it's cut from the nicest cloth, heartfelt thanks, Mr Zweig, and above all follow my advice, forget about all the articles that accused you of betraying your host country. Don't believe a word they say: 'Zweig sold his pen for a visa', or those who maintain that *Brazil, Land of the Future* was commissioned by the government. No, you're not a propagandist working for our great President Vargas—may God watch over his soul—all those who speak about you like that are nothing but malicious gossips. You're goodness personified."

She grabbed the autographed handkerchief and returned to her table.

He had grown sombre and was staring into space. Lotte waved a hand in front of his eyes.

"You see? It's wonderful, you're just as famous here as in Vienna!"

He suggested they go back home.

*

The doorbell echoed in the silent dusk. He heard the house-keeper's footsteps in the corridor. He overheard a commotion and turned his head.

"Happy birthday, Stefan!"

They had all gathered in the entrance to the lounge: Abrahão Koogan and his wife, Cláudio de Souza, the chair of Brazilian PEN, as well as Ernst Feder and wife—Feder was the former editor-in-chief of the *Berliner Tageblatt* and had recently moved into the house next door. Stefan stood up and embraced his friends one after the other as Lotte looked on from a corner of the room, slightly removed from the commotion. This little party to celebrate Stefan's sixtieth birthday had been her idea, which she'd hatched in secret over a long period of time. She had hesitated and had even abandoned her plans on a number of occasions. She recalled his words on the matter: "We don't have the right to be happy in times like this, neither as men nor as Jews. We're neither better nor more precious than those of us still being hunted down in Europe." Throughout the week leading up to the party, she had employed a number of ruses in order to make the necessary arrangements. She feared how he might react—he didn't like surprises and he loathed being feted. On top of that, he abhorred the idea of celebrating his sixtieth birthday. The contrast between his fiftieth and sixtieth birthdays was startling. That decade had seen him transported from a realm of light into one of darkness. On his fiftieth, Stefan had received tons of letters from friends and readers from across the world at his home in Kapuzinerberg. Whereas today he had no fixed address and all his books had gone up in smoke. The 28th of November 1941 terrorized him. He was sixty. He felt he was getting old. A few more months and he would have outlived his father. His friends Ernst Weiss, Erwin Rieger and Ernst Toller had decided to put an end to their lives, while others had either been murdered or were rotting away in Dachau. Happy birthday? He hadn't wanted to spend the day at home. He had accepted Lotte's suggestion that he visit Teresópolis, fifty kilometres north of Rio. They had strolled along the pavements of the city, which was nestled on a mountainside. They had seen the peaks and valleys of the Serra dos Órgãos stretching out as far as the eye could see from every street corner. They had stopped at a restaurant on the Avenida Feliciano-Sodré. It had been a pleasant day. They'd had no reason be to be afraid. On their return, towards the end of the afternoon, he had found a present on top of the table in the lounge, a present that had thrilled him. How on earth had she found Balzac's collected works at the antiquarian bookseller's on Rua São José? Although the edition was several decades old, it was complete. He had seen this as a good omen. Balzac had found his way to him. Perhaps all the notes he had collected on the Frenchman in London would also be in his hands soon enough. He had reasons to hope.

Once he'd embraced all his guests, it was time to open his presents. Ernst Feder was the first up, with a leather-bound volume of Montaigne's works.

"Here you are, my dear Stefan, may his wisdom dispel all your dark thoughts…"

Then came Abrahão Koogan's turn. A little dog jumped out of the half-open knapsack he was holding in his hand. The fox terrier triggered a wave of laughter when he licked the legs of the assembled guests. De Souza presented him with a paperback edition of *Brazil, Land of the Future* inscribed with birthday greetings from Soarès, the foreign minister.

Next the housekeeper handed him the dozen telegrams that had arrived at the house during the day. Lotte slipped away when her husband started reading a telex his ex-wife had sent him from New York. She returned a moment later bearing what she knew was the most wonderful present of them all: a parcel from Jules Romains, which had arrived the previous day. From his base in New York, his French friend had put together a *Festschrift*, a celebratory book assembled in the traditional German manner— a glorious gift with which to commemorate a birthday. It was a limited edition of the texts given at the conference that the French author had convened in Paris in 1939 entitled "Stefan Zweig: A Great European". Its fifty pages sketched a laudatory portrait of the Viennese humanist and came in two volumes, one of which was leather-bound and in French, printed by Éditions de la Maison Française, and the other of which was in English. Jules Romains's book moved Stefan to tears. Friderike was forgotten!

Feder leafed through the book. "Now you can die in peace," he said. "They've already printed your obituary."

They dined on a roast served with potatoes on the side, which had been prepared according to a European recipe that Lotte had taught Rosaria, although it had come out a little too spicy and undercooked. When it was time for dessert, Lotte was briefly tempted to open the bottle of champagne that Feder had brought. Yet she remembered her husband's words: "Jews have nothing to celebrate these days, surviving is the best they can hope for." No, champagne would be over the top.

When the meal was over, he stood up and went to his desk to pick up a slightly rumpled sheet of paper that had been scribbled on. He then returned to the table and tinkled his glass with a spoon to obtain everyone's silence. He reassured his audience that his speech would not be overly long. He began by thanking everyone present. He unfolded the sheet of paper and explained that he'd composed a poem to mark his birthday and he asked his audience to indulge him. He hadn't written any poetry for a long time, and this would undoubtedly be his last. The poem's only real merit was that it voiced his current state of being as faithfully as possible. Stefan put his spectacles on and began to read. His voice trembled, but his eyes were dry—that was the most important thing.

'A MAN OF SIXTY GIVES THANKS'

The hours dance more gently now
That years to come are few.
For only when the wine runs low
The golden glass shows through.

Presentiments of closing day,
When our desires are gone,
Soothe us far more than they dismay
Now, in the setting sun.

We do not ask what we did right
Or what was not done well.
And growing old is but the light
Prelude to our farewell.

The world before us never lay
So fair, or life so true,
As in the glow of parting day,
When shadows dim the view.

A silence fell over the room. The audience seemed perplexed. Stefan folded the sheet, put it in his pocket and sat down. Lotte rose abruptly and hurried off to her bedroom, her eyes wet with tears. Feder quipped:

"You might be well advised to stick to prose… considering the effect your poems have on your loved ones."

Stefan excused himself, took his leave and went to join his wife. He sat on the bed, beside the weeping Lotte. He whispered a few soothing words, pulled out a handkerchief and dried her cheeks and forehead. In a choked voice, she looked right into his eyes and said:

"I don't want to live in this world without you. I would follow you into the afterlife, don't leave me alone!"

He replied that he'd never leave her behind. She could follow him wherever he went.

Those words assuaged Lotte's distress. Her sobs dried up and he told her he would be rejoining their guests, suggesting she might like to follow him soon. She concurred, kissed him on the lips, grasped his hand and held him tightly in her arms. He had to go back to the lounge. He walked past the mirror on his way out and smoothed a loose lock of hair into place. He wondered whether his hair would soon fall out, just like his teeth had. He was an old man. He straightened his jacket and left the bedroom. Once back with his guests, he adopted the fixed, slightly vapid smile he usually wore during social occasions, which he thought made him look light-hearted and laid back.

Before retiring, he went to the bathroom to pick up his sleeping pills, as he did every night. He emptied three capsules out of the bottle and swallowed them with a little water, replaced the lid, changed his mind, and then doubled the dose.

That night, his mother appeared to him in his sleep. She was pacing up and down the long corridors of the apartment at 17 Rathausstrasse. She was fanning herself gracefully. She wore a long, dark velvet dress. As usual, her high heels didn't impede her walking and gave the impression she was far taller than her actual height, which was five foot two. She drew nearer, looking radiant, an array of jewels around her neck and bracelets jingling on her wrists. Stefan, a child, was sitting on the floor wearing navy shorts and a striped shirt that she'd picked out for him. He watched her walk by, at a loss as to what to say to make her linger. He ate alone with his brother that evening, like they did every evening. Once she'd walked past, Stefan couldn't refrain from getting up and running after her to offer up his cheek for a kiss. She pretended to ignore him and kept on walking, without looking back. Once she had reached the end of the corridor, she ordered him back to his room. What was he doing sitting on the floor? That was no way for a Zweig to behave! He started running after her, running until he was out of breath, and when his fingers grazed the fabric of her dress, his world would suddenly fill with a bright light. His mother was stretched out on her bed, her hair had gone white and her skin had lost its former lustre. She didn't acknowledge him in any way. Her eyes were glum and weary. She had lost her hearing. Her cheeks were sunken and her face was pale. He drew near to caress her arm and his hand wandered in the void. He puckered his lips and his mouth kissed the void.

He woke up with a start, drenched in sweat.

He hadn't been able to close his mother's eyes when she'd died. He hadn't recited the Kaddish. He hadn't fulfilled the most important commandment that all Jewish children were bound by. By the time Ida Zweig breathed her last in August 1938, he had long since fled Austria and had been denied permission to return and be by his mother's bedside. German troops had entered Vienna on 13th March 1938. It had taken only six months for barbarism to be unleashed on the Jews. His mother, an eighty-four-year-old invalid who was hard of hearing, had suffered the worst humiliations. During the early days of the *Anschluss*, she had witnessed her son's books burning on the pyres that had been erected on Viennese squares. If that old lady had been able to muster the requisite strengths to stroll through the Prater's gardens, she would have been forbidden, under penalty of death, to sit on one of the park benches. It hadn't taken long for her to fall ill. Cousin Egon was granted permission to visit her, but only once a day. Despite costing an arm and a leg, an Aryan nurse had been engaged and given the adjacent room to sleep in. Yet since an Aryan couldn't sleep under the same roof as a Jew, Egon had been forbidden to remain by Ida's side during those final nights, when her end had loomed in sight.

Ida Zweig had died alone on a summer night in 1938. Stefan had felt almost relieved when he'd heard the news. The Nazis had managed to ensure a son would feel relieved by his own mother's death. At least she had been spared from suffering further abuses and unspeakable cruelties. A few months later, they had forced all the Jews in Vienna to vacate their flats, relocating them outside the Ring, cramming entire families into dilapidated houses. In the space of a year, Vienna had been cleansed of all its Jews.

Although he had given eulogies for so many of his loved ones, from Rilke to Freud, he hadn't recited the Kaddish for his mother. But he didn't know how to pray in Hebrew. His parents hadn't wanted him to learn the language of his ancestors. Who cared about being Jewish in Vienna back then?

DECEMBER

THE SPIRIT OF THE ENLIGHTENMENT had loomed over the hills ever since Ernst Feder had arrived in Petrópolis. The man had been in charge of the *Berliner Tageblatt*, a distinguished newspaper. Prior to the advent of fascism, the neighbours had met one another numerous times in Berlin. Feder had been proud to list Stefan Zweig among his occasional columnists for his literary pages. Whom hadn't he written for since his first review had been published in Herzl's *Neue Freie Presse* in 1901? He had written for every paper and magazine Europe had to offer, praising renowned writers to the skies or introducing emerging talents. Stefan's own critical reception had been far from welcoming. They had reproached him for his lifelessness and his flippant flights of fancy, only then to seek his support. That travelling circus seemed so shallow and far-removed today.

On some nights he had dined with Feder at the Café Élégant, a restaurant whose tables were arranged at the bottom of Rua Dias. It was a tiny greasy spoon with a frontage that was only a few feet wide, but they offered a variety of dishes besides black beans on their menu and their coffee was better than any he'd had in Vienna. Seated on that terrace in front of a friend who spoke his language, Stefan felt as though he'd stepped back in time.

He was very fond of Feder. He had missed his sense of humour, as well as his cool, detached way of looking at world events. He had the ability to make light of one's worst fears. He was quintessentially German in that way and every inch a Jew. "I remain a natural optimist," he would dare to say. "Considering the recent turn of events, the Reich is definitely not going to be around for a thousand years. I give them five hundred years at the most... Come on, I guarantee you that just as fervently as I once expressed it to Walter Benjamin: we have no reason to despair!" By what accident of history had the Austrian writer and the journalist from Berlin found themselves in the middle of that valley surrounded by the jungle? They talked about the past. They talked about literature. They evaluated the comparative merits of Heine and Schiller, chatted about Goethe and Nietzsche. They tallied the books they'd been able to take into exile with them. They argued over the "Young Vienna" school. They mused about whether writers like Schnitzler, Hofmannsthal, Rilke, Wassermann and Hesse were still worth reading. Yet they never broached the subject of which of these would be remembered by posterity. They never talked about the future. There was no future in this place. Even the present seemed a little unreal. There they were, just the two of them, like a decade earlier, except that creepers had entwined themselves around the café's sign. The cries of monkeys emerged from the nearby jungle. No, it wasn't Vienna. They were neither at the Café Central nor at the Café Museum. Petrópolis looked like a ghost city and they were the ghosts. It would have come as no surprise to Stefan had the trees and the mountains started to move and darkness engulfed the earth and the sky.

When their talk shifted to current events, the conversation quickly ran out of steam. They became as silent as though they'd been watching a funeral procession march by. After which they asked the café owner to bring them a chessboard. They began to play. Stefan was a mediocre player, even though he had recently picked up a little book that summarized the games played by the greatest grandmasters, a book he'd brought with him from New York without really knowing why. He had begun reading it on the boat that had brought them to Brazil and a new idea had come to him. He didn't know what he would do with this story once he'd finished writing it. The plot had taken shape, at first in his head, then the words had come to him, almost effortlessly. He had never been prey to writer's block. He would have certainly preferred to be better acquainted with the agonies of writing. He wrote like he thought. He sketched out the characters quickly, adventures would pop up in his mind and the plots, which were all alike, would begin to take shape. He would have loved to plumb the depths of souls a little longer and a little deeper, but after a few weeks he had always come to the conclusion that he'd exhausted all of his material. In the end, they were all invariably similar to one another: short stories about single-minded passions, irrepressible loves and macabre consequences. Everything was irremediably greedy and exuberant—in other words, the complete opposite of his own character. His work lit a succession of conflagrations in the hearts of his heroes, who would throw themselves head first into the flames while he burned on the inside. Indeed, when it came to the subjects of his stories, it was always the same old tune. The characters would attempt to resist their passions and once they relented and gave in to them, their guilty consciences prompted them either to turn their backs on life or to lapse into madness. As far as he was concerned, his work was governed by an overly simplistic mechanism: the fires of passion and the flames of hell. He reproached himself for never having scratched past the emotional surface of things, of never having struck the right tone, yes, that's right, that was the reason he'd never been able to write anything but short stories. He'd never had the courage to plumb the depths of his characters. He had never accomplished the feat of narrating an entire life. He'd never written a masterpiece, a voluminous, heavy novel, something both dense and pacey, like *Berlin Alexanderplatz* and *The Magic Mountain*… Klaus Mann and Ernst Weiss had been right to mock him. He was nothing but a minor writer, a dilettante, a mundane chronicler, an inveterate bourgeois who hadn't suffered for his art. As for his current heroes, the chess players, he still had no idea of what would happen to them, but Dr B. would undoubtedly discover the destinies of all the other characters would lead to either death or suicide.

One evening, Feder had confided in him: "Well, I've lost my house, my country, my newspaper and I don't know whether most of my family has managed to find a safe haven, but I've got a good reason to be satisfied with my condition: imagine the book I'll be able to write once all this is over. I picture it as a sort of *Robinson Crusoe*, but one that speaks to the German-Jewish experience and is told through the eyes of Friday. Yes, I'll be Friday, and since the fate of Jews everywhere is hanging in the balance, I'll call myself Saturday, yes, Sabbath will be my pseudonym, an illustrious, holy name. I will be Sabbath and I will live on an island alongside the great Crusozweig. My book will tell the story of this Crusozweig, alone in the middle of the jungle. Put your mind at ease, I'm not taking any notes. I've inscribed everything on my memory. I can see the title on the jacket cover: *Five Years with Stefan Zweig*—yes, I share your natural optimism, of course the war won't be over until 1946 or 1947. I've already got the climax in mind, it will be a chapter called 'The Day that Zweig Smiled'. But the chapter entitled 'The Day Zweig Shed a Tear' will also be good… We'll hit the lecture circuit. You'll stand beside me and all you'll have to do is nod your head. My book will cast the spotlight on you. I will reveal that you are in fact quite a jolly man, always up for a laugh, easy to get on with, that you see life through rose-tinted glasses and that you want nothing out of life other than to smoke a fine cigar. Yes, I, Ernst Feder, will be the biographer of the man who will become the first Jewish Nobel laureate as soon as the war is over! Fine, I forgot about Bergson, but was Bergson really a writer?…"

Feder was being sarcastic of course. He was well acquainted with Stefan's novels and his comments had always provided welcome encouragement. With a trusted reader like Feder, he felt himself becoming a writer again, in short, he finally felt like himself again. He rediscovered his identity. He was able to escape the punishment of exile.

"What I really like about you," Feder explained, "is your Freudian undertone. Exactly, Freudian. You're not a storyteller. You use a narrator to give an account and this narrator interacts with an outsider, who in turns hears the narrator's confession. You have taken the technique of the embedded narrative to unparalleled heights. You have invented the literary psychoanalytical novel. You are Freud's alter ego, not Schnitzler. As far as I'm concerned, what's really interesting about your books is the relationship between the narrator and the interlocutor. I'm fascinated more by this confessor than by your heroes, this being who remains in the shadows and who never passes judgement. Unlike most writers, you're never the hero of your own books. Your 'I' is like a ghost inside this being who is the repository of all the world's miseries… Your novels won't be remembered for the way they evoke the world of yesterday, that dear forgotten world of yours, but as the chronicle of a carnage. You're fooling yourself if you hope to be remembered as the master storyteller of the old gilt days or the great bard of nostalgia. The characters in your books are a testament to the destruction of the world… and please forgive my bluntness here but your heroes only ever talk about your own wound and they chronicle every stage of your long downward spiral. You shy away from activism, refuse to sign our petitions or fight with the exile organizations, you once even placed your hopes in Chamberlain, which goes to show, doesn't it? But your fight lies elsewhere, you're engaged in documenting the destruction of the world. You had so assimilated yourself into that Viennese world, that dear departed Mitteleuropean culture, that when the Nazis destroyed it, you got torn apart in the process. What you describe, as though you'd foreseen it, and what your books express, through the madness of your heroes, is the story of your own annihilation—and this story is so intense and candid, your writing is so painstaking and crisp, that your work and your personality have blended seamlessly into one. Your characters never stood a chance. They were doomed as soon as they opened their mouths or exchanged a first glance with someone. You lead them to the place where you have spent the entirety of your life… under the rubble. I don't know whether this is a divine gift or a hellish curse. The Nazis are the embodiment of evil, while you're catastrophe personified. You're the writer of disaster… All right, now where was I? You moved your bishop to d6, didn't you?… So I'll move my queen to c7. I've got one word for you: checkmate!"

*

Lotte was running down Avenida Kocler, blue in the face. Whenever she found herself gasping for air, she would put down her basket loaded with fruit and vegetables at the foot of a tree.

Let the children help themselves to it! Let them throw a street party in the city square! Let the women wear their jewels and the men crack open bottles of champagne! This day was a great day. This day would be remembered for ever as the most celebrated day in the history of mankind. Light had come back to earth. God had broken through the silence. America was entering the war! She had just heard the news. The historic event was on the front pages of all the dailies featured in the news-stand on the market square. She had read and reread all the headlines to make sure she wasn't hallucinating. The news-stand owner had assured her she wasn't dreaming: Roosevelt had declared war on Germany and Japan. Tremble with fear Hitler, your days are numbered!

In a month's time, the Flying Fortresses she had seen on the newsreels would descend on Europe. Armadas of ships would unleash millions of GIs on the beaches of the Atlantic coast. The soldiers of Liberty would have the German butchers for breakfast! The forces of Good would vanquish the demons. They were saved! Jews would be celebrating this day in Katowice, Frankfurt and Vienna, singing hymns to the Lord! Their ordeal had come to an end. America had reached out its hand to the damned. Quick, she had to give Stefan the news! He wouldn't have heard it. He had recently decided to stop reading newspapers and listening to the radio. He could no longer put up with the bulletins of tragedies and catastrophes getting in the way of his work. He had sequestered himself. But he had started writing again. He had finished his *Montaigne*, had just put the finishing touches on his story about chess players and had begun a novel whose heroine was called Clarissa—Clarissa, what an odd idea! He had come to terms with the madness of men. But today the tide had finally turned. A new era had been ushered in. The time of solitude and chaos was a thing of the past. Tomorrow,

Brazil would rally around the United States and men throughout the Americas would enlist and board ships destined for Europe. Victories would come thick and fast and entire populations would rise up and rebel against the German butchers. The troops of the Reich would desert en masse. It was 1941 and the war was over! In two months' time, soldiers would cross the Rhine. In three, they would lay siege to Vienna and Frankfurt. Berlin would fall into the hands of the Allies. Yes, by July 1942 crowds of ecstatic Jews would dance the old Jewish dances around the soldiers and sing hymns to the Lord and Franklin Delano Roosevelt, may God bless that saintly man. They were saved! Next year in Vienna! Yes, she would walk along the Ring arm in arm with her husband. They would be welcomed at the Central Station in Vienna by a horde of journalists. A flurry of camera flashes. "Mr and Mrs Zweig have arrived in Vienna," the photo captions would read. "Above, Mrs Lotte Zweig joins her husband at the Beethoven Café." For the first time, they would walk side by side down the pathways of the Schönbrunn garden. Make their rounds through the Prater's park. She would walk up the steps of the Burgtheater leaning on his arm. In order to celebrate the return of the city's prodigal son, the mayor would decide to schedule a new performance of *Jeremiah*. During the premiere, the audience would give him a standing ovation, applauding the author as he walked onto the stage... alongside his young wife. They would sleep in the royal suite at the Hotel Continental. They would dine at Sluka. Then they would treat themselves to *Sachertorte* at Demel. Walking past the bookshops on the Burggasse, they would spot Stefan Zweig's books in prominent places on all the shelves. Men would tip their hats in the street. They would express delight at their return. They had waited too long to do so—and why had they even left in the first place? Had Vienna ever stopped being the city of lights?

They had to be patient, hold on for another six or seven months. After all, she was only thirty years old. If she looked ten years older, it was because of her illness and the pressures of life in exile. In Vienna, she would recover her youth and be known as the stylish Mrs Zweig. Who knows, perhaps some men might even decide to pay her court? Yes, the idea of being seduced delighted her. Glory to the Lord and glory to America which had given beauty back to the exiles! A reception would be given in Zweig's honour in the great hall of the Opera. Theirs would be the first dance of the ball. They would dance, solemnly, as if they were the only couple in the world, ignoring the others as they looked on. Perhaps as other couples began to join in and as euphoria filled the room, Stefan might lean over and whisper, "I love you, Lotte… I love you," into her ear. It would be the first time she'd ever heard him utter that phrase, and those words would be meant solely for her, Elizabeth Charlotte Zweig, and nobody else. Maybe she would pretend not to hear him? She would make him repeat it and Zweig's lips would part again to mouth those words. She would heap blessings upon the Lord, the king of the universe, who in his great clemency had finally allowed that moment to come. Amen.

She climbed the slope that led to the house, so cheerful that she was oblivious to her panting. She was drenched in sweat and gasping for air, thanks to all that crazy running under the midday sun. What did she care? They were saved. Hallelujah! They were going to live! The 8th of December 1941. They weren't alone any more.

She caught her breath before going in. To curb her enthusiasm. She felt feverish. She was in such a hurry to see a smile light her beloved's face. As soon as she gave him the news, he would no doubt embrace her and plant a kiss on her lips. Perhaps—though she preferred not to get her hopes up—he might lead her into the bedroom and they would make love right there and then, in that place, on that day, and yes, she would give birth to a child nine months later while on a ship back to Europe. She bit her lips so as not to scream with joy. She was going to be a mother!

She opened the door and took a few steps down the corridor. Her husband's shadow loomed over the veranda. He was sitting in his armchair and appeared to be dozing. Or maybe he was in the midst of daydreaming about Clarissa, or his impossibly difficult *Balzac*. "You'll be able to resume work on your masterpiece. The oceans will soon be safe to cross. Your precious research will leave London, cross the oceans and reach safety. You'll have finished your *Balzac* before V-Day. The war is over, over!"

She walked on her tiptoes until she was right in front of him. No, he wasn't sleeping. On seeing her, he smiled, using the same forced smile that no longer fooled her. At the exact moment when she'd opened her mouth to give him the news, her eyes had fallen on that day's newspaper spread out over his knees, with its jubilant banner headline. Her eyes drifted back to her husband. The man remained impassive. Something shattered inside her. She was assailed by a feeling of great distress and confusion. How could he cling to that sad expression when the end of the nightmare had been announced? What more could he possibly want? The Resurrection of the Dead?

In a voice that still betrayed some of its former excitement, she asked:

"Have you heard the news?"

He nodded.

"Isn't it a great day?"

He agreed that it was.

"I feel like singing and dancing…"

He told her she was right, that it was a great day. He had also felt elated that morning when Feder had come to bring him the newspaper.

"But you don't seem…?"

Sure, he was happy, but she knew how he was, he'd never been very effusive. She knelt before him, took his hand in hers and kissed it; then, moved to tears, she murmured:

"We're saved, isn't that so? We're saved…"

He kissed her fingers, ran his fingers through her hair and grasped her face between his hands. Yes, she was right, they were saved. At which point he asked her if she could leave him alone. He had to work. She got up, dried her tear-drenched face, headed towards the door and left.

I am cursed, my name is cursed, curse the day I set foot inside that office in London, the office of that great Austrian Writer, that man, that doom-monger, who is incapable of experiencing happiness. I should leave this place, yes, find salvation in escape, but where would I go? He's led me to this prison where there are creepers instead of bears, he's carried me off to the other side of the world and I've got nowhere to go, no one who's waiting for me, I am forced to stay here, beside this marble-like being, in this tomb of unhappiness, oh yes, that's why he's chosen this place, a necropolis, an imperial city without an empire. I would have loved to live in New York, to stay with Eva, she and I would have danced on this day, right on Fifth Avenue, where all Jews must now be dancing, because this day is a great day, the war is over and the Lord has shown us the way, the Lord will lead us out of Germany just like he led us out of Egypt. Hitler isn't a more formidable foe than the Pharaoh, our ordeal is at an end, the Lord has forgiven our sins and He once again holds His hand out to His people. Yet Stefan is obviously incapable of rejoicing, since he believes in nothing, neither in God, nor in Roosevelt. Death is Stefan Zweig's only companion.

He had kept the truth from her. He hadn't wanted to inflict the story that Feder had told him that very morning. He hadn't wanted to spoil her happiness. He would tell her all about it later, or, seeing as she was so fragile, maybe he wouldn't say anything at all. He needed to protect her. Who knew how she might react? Yes, he had to warn Feder against saying anything —and if they managed to keep it quiet, she would never find out. The newspapers didn't report those kinds of atrocities.

Feder had dropped by mid morning carrying a newspaper under his arm.

"I have some good news and some unimaginably bad news. Let's start with the good... Here you go, read this... but don't get ahead of yourself and cheer up too quickly."

He had scanned the headlines and had suddenly felt pure and intense joy course through him, a feeling he hadn't experienced for many years, a feeling that was a mix of drunkenness and relief. This state of emotion must have been clearly visible on his face since Feder had immediately jumped in and said:

"No, I told you, you're going to regret getting so excited. Come to your senses and readopt your gloomy disposition because now you're going to listen to what I have to tell you..."

Feder had been woken at dawn by a phone call. Albert Seldmann, a spokesman for one of the exile organizations, had rung him from New York. His voice had trembled. He had punctuated his remarks with a recurring phrase:

"All of this has been verified, you hear me, Ernst, this is the undiluted truth."

During the first days of November, they had rounded up hundreds of Jews in each city of the Reich and herded them into big public squares. It had started with the Jews in Hamburg and the following day it had been the turn of those in Frankfurt, Bremen, then Berlin, and finally Vienna and Salzburg. They had marched the Jews to the railway stations, and after all those months of death, privations and humiliations, they had loaded them onto the trains. Once the compartments had been packed full, the trains had started off. They had crossed Germany and occupied Poland and come to a stop in Minsk. The first convoy had arrived on 10th November. All of this has been verified, this is the undiluted truth. A thousand Jews from Hamburg had been dragged to a place where the sign above the entrance had read "*Sonderghetto*", which had been specially erected for the ghetto in Minsk. Three days after the thousand Jews from Hamburg had arrived, they had been joined by five thousand more from Frankfurt. All of this has been verified. On 18th November, a convoy from the capital had unloaded its first shipment of Jews from Berlin. That was on the same day that the first Jews from Vienna had also arrived. Three hundred Viennese Jews. In preparation for the coming influx of German Jews, all the Jews had been cleared out of the large ghetto in Minsk in order to make room for all the Reich's Jews. They had killed ten thousand Jews over the space of five days.

This is what Albert Seldmann had told him that morning.

Feder had stopped, fixed his gaze upon his interlocutor, and then resumed:

"Do you remember that terrible novel of Bettauer's called *The City Without Jews?*"

Zweig replied that he did. The book dated from the 1920s.

He had picked it up because the author's name, Bettauer, had reminded him of his mother's name. He had read the book and hated it. The novel told a story in which Vienna's inhabitants had expelled the Jews from the city in the name of Aryan purity. It had been an unqualified success and Bettauer had been assassinated two years following its publication.

"Well, here we are faced with same scenario," Feder said. "The Reich is going to be cleansed of all its Jews… At this rate, there won't be a single Jew left in Germany in a year's time, including Vienna, of course. Can you imagine it? Not a single Jew left in Vienna or Berlin. Not a single Jew left in the whole of Germany. How is it conceivable?"

Feder stood up, turned on his heels, went away, then came back and broke into sobs in his host's arms. While he consoled his visitor, Stefan counted the number of relatives he still had in Vienna. Nineteen cousins. Then he spared a thought for Lotte's grandfather, the rabbi of Frankfurt.

*

From that moment on, he spent most of his time at home, sitting behind his makeshift desk and writing, mechanically and uninspired. He wrote like Roth used to drink, joylessly and effortlessly. He was jotting down ideas on a number of loose sheets.

Compile a yearbook of life in exile over the years 1941 and 1942 that will include a selection of the best work by émigré writers and show they are still productive. A German yearbook with Thomas and Heinrich Mann and an Austrian yearbook with Werfel and Beer-Hofmann. A French yearbook with Maurois, Bernanos, Jules Romains and Pierre Cot. Set up a coordinating committee in New York to be headed by Klaus Mann. Talk it over with Bruno Kreitner.

He had abandoned work on his *Balzac*. He would never be up to the task. He had lost all hope that the suitcase full of papers from London would ever reach him. The ship that had been carrying it was undoubtedly lying at the bottom of the ocean, sunk by a German U-boat. Whenever he started on new stories and wrote the first few pages, he quickly tore them up. He vainly hoped to be hit by a lightning bolt of inspiration, something of the euphoria that had once gripped him every time he'd picked up a pen. Nothing sang in his soul any more.

He'd got worked up about an idea for a new novel, an ambitious project that would encompass the first half of the century and encapsulate an entire epoch, which would talk about the two wars, serve as the equivalent of an autobiography, but of course under the guise of fiction. He had begun writing it a few weeks earlier. The story commenced in 1902. It was narrated by a woman, who was also the novel's heroine. He was satisfied with the first chapters. Yes, the book held up between 1902 and 1914. Clarissa came across as lively, affectionate, compassionate and integrated. The book was taking shape. The hundred or so pages he'd already written were a promise of things to come.

Then he suddenly lost his train of thought. His heroine's characteristics faded away. Clarissa became a stranger to him. Sometimes she came across like Christine, the post-office girl, while at others she resembled Irene, the protagonist of *Fear*. Soon enough, the novel lost all semblance of a narrative structure. It didn't look like anything any more. The chapter that covered the year 1919 came to only six pages. The section regarding the following two years amounted to only three… here is how he had described the 1920s:

These were the dead years for Clarissa. Her child was the only thing she had in the world.

That was his masterpiece! The same man who had needed fifty thousand words to narrate *Twenty-Four Hours in the Life of a Woman* had now reduced ten years of someone's life to a couple of sentences. He felt pathetic. He remembered the time when an inexhaustible stream had flowed effortlessly out of him. Worlds had been built and characters brought to life. How easy it had been for him to plumb the depths of their souls! He had looked into their pasts and foretold their futures. When he used to sit at his desk, pick up his pen and watch the miracle occur right in front of his eyes—oh, those moments when dawn would sneak up on him after a night's work in Salzburg! These days, both his mind and his inkwell had dried up. Words evaded him and his characters slipped from his fingers. A doomsday atmosphere reigned over his inner world. There were no characters left in his mind, no children were born and no women smiled. The heart of mankind had stopped beating. His mind was a mirror image of the world of Jews. A land buried beneath smouldering ashes.

*

There was a knock at the door. Lotte ran to answer it, rapt by the idea that a visitor might help dispel the day's gloominess. She thought she recognized the man standing on the front steps, but she could not recall his name. The man introduced himself. Lotte suddenly felt her spirits sink to new-found depths as she coldly ushered the visitor in and announced him, at which point she vanished into her room. Siegfried Burger, Friderike's brother, who had been living in exile in Rio for the past few weeks, had come to pay his former brother-in-law a visit.

She heard the outburst of joy through the door. The pair must have fallen into one another's arms. Stefan's voice sounded uncharacteristically happy and enthusiastic. He showered questions upon his visitor, wanting to know how he'd managed to get to Rio. Where had he fled from? Which route had he taken? How had he obtained a visa? Was the visa provisional? Where was he staying in Rio? At which point he broke into a torrent of words and began reminiscing about the past, talking about shared memories, remembering their walks in the Belvedere, receptions at the Hofburg, dinners in town, all the weeks, months and years they'd lived during Vienna's halcyon days.

The physical resemblance between brother and sister was shocking. It was as if Friderike was in the next room. Lotte didn't want to give up without a fight. She went back into the lounge.

When she stepped into the room, the men didn't break off their conversation. Her presence didn't disturb them reminiscing about a past from which she was excluded. She brought them tea and they thanked her, yet however warmly they did so, it seemed as though they were speaking to someone else. They were in Kapuzinerberg now and it was Friderike who was pouring them refreshments. Lotte observed her husband. His face had changed. His disposition had changed. His posture was straight and the tone of his voice was more assertive. He had transformed back into the married man whom she'd met seven years ago. Siegfried Burger had come into the house and Friderike (née Burger) had gained a foothold in the lounge. Siegfried had sat down on the worn leather armchair and Friderike was standing behind him. Lotte felt like a third wheel. Her heart skipped a beat when she heard her husband enquire after his ex-wife. When he asked Siegfried whether he missed his sister, he added in a choked voice that he missed her too. She took a step in the direction of the corridor. Pretending not to have heard Stefan's question, Siegfried held Lotte back. He announced that he had brought a letter with him that, he said, turning to face her, "will make you happy". Lotte's rage subsided. The letter was addressed to "Stefan and Lotte". Siegfried read it out loud. It began with a protracted passage in which Friderike related how happy she was to be in New York and free at last. How she had narrowly avoided being arrested along with her daughters at the port in Marseilles. She said she felt good in New York. She no longer felt nostalgic about Austria. She had been campaigning for the United States to enter the war on Britain's side, but these days she spent most of her time at the Bureau of Immigration on Ellis Island. She had regained her faith in the future in that New World, where people looked and spoke to you without hatred. As Siegfried read those sentences out, Lotte noticed a trace of disappointment flicker past Stefan's eyes. Happy… without him? Siegfried interrupted his reading and, addressing Lotte, said: "This is the part that's going to interest you…" He resumed reading the letter. Friderike had hosted Eva Altmann—Eva, her niece!—for two weeks, having found her in a youth hostel. Eva and Friderike had had a marvellous time; "that young girl is wonderful," the letter said. They had gone to Coney Island, strolled along the beach at Long Island where they had taken their first dip in the ocean: "Rest assured, dear Lotte, that I am looking after her and that we will one day experience again those marvellous moments together." Lotte felt a jolt of happiness. Then she felt a violent pang of pain. Her gaze drifted off to the world outside the window. Evening was fast approaching and a mist was settling over the town and the valley. She couldn't tear her eyes away from that dismal scene. The image of happy crowds strolling the streets of New York had taken over her mind. Was the world really divided between people who were happy and those who were cursed?

JANUARY

T HEY LED A PEACEFUL LIFE. Compared to the rising pile
of corpses, it was a relatively normal existence. The news of
calamities only reached them sporadically. Their fate was sealed and
their eyelids were nearly shut. Nothing would ever come and clear
the piles of corpses away. They would no longer live in fear. Silence
would reign all around them. They had built a lonely world for
themselves. Each day, they set themselves the task of forgetting. They
no longer listened to the radio, didn't read the newspapers, avoided
their friends and allowed the telephone to ring off the hook. They
rarely opened their front door and left their post unopened. They
didn't write any more letters, took no trains and left the house as little
as possible. Their entire life played out between those whitewashed
walls. It was a closed world, where it was often difficult to breathe
and the air felt like dust. They too would revert to dust. They never
raised their voices, never lifted their gaze, their souls were no longer
familiar with either joy or distress. Their hearts had simply stopped
beating. They lived their life as if they were ghosts. Sleep eluded
them. The world's miseries no longer reverberated in their ears. The
memory of their loved ones had evaporated. Oblivion was their only
companion. They no longer participated in the world. They were
no longer Jewish, no longer Austrian, no longer German. They had
cheated destiny. Their fortress was impregnable. They had won.

But one day a rumble would fill the air. Darkness would streak the sky. Sirens would blare out. The earth would be blown apart. Giant aircraft with swastikas on their wings would drop their bombs. The earth would be set ablaze, houses would burn and the streets would be strewn with mangled bodies. Armoured infantry would fire their cannon across Rio's bay. Thousands of soldiers would spill out of ships and swarm over Copacabana beach. The Wehrmacht would march along the Avenida Rio Branco. The generals would take over city hall. They would post their decrees on the walls of each avenue and those of the *favelas*. The SS would disperse throughout the city in small detachments looting palaces and homes. The window displays of department stores would be covered with yellow stars. They would order exiles to register with the authorities. They would insist on taking a census of native Jews. They would enact the racial laws. Then the hunting season would start. First they would imprison all the German refugees, after which they would move on to noteworthy local Jews before starting to round up families. Black-shirted men with machine guns in hand and rabid dogs frothing at the mouth on a leash would burst into schools looking for Jewish children. Once Rio had been cleansed, the SS would advance farther north along the highway. Petrópolis would be their first port of call. They would seal off Avenida Koeler and begin their manhunt. They would easily track him down to 94 Rua Gonçalves Dias. They would break down the door. They would point their guns at them and force them to leave the house. They would make them climb into a curtain-sided lorry. They would then drive them down into the valley, just like they'd done with those women and children in the forests of Poland. In the little jungle close to Teresópolis, they would put a bullet in his head. After that it would be Lotte's turn.

Brazil, land of the future?

*

The housekeeper announced a visitor. A man in a dark suit with a thin, misshapen chestnut beard and a black hat on his head came into the lounge.

"Rabbi Hemle, Henrique Hemle."

His handshake was firm, his gaze was thoughtful, intense and affable. The man must have been in his forties, but his features were lit by a boyish spark. His voice was gentle. In a fluent, elegant German he explained that he had made the trip from Rio specifically to meet his host and apologized for the intrusion, hoping that he hadn't arrived at an inappropriate time.

Stefan shook his head and replied that he wasn't worth such a journey.

"The journey had been long overdue," the rabbi said. "I had already travelled once to hear you speak and catch a glimpse of you. That was back in 1923, in the wake of my bar mitzvah. My father, who was one of your devoted readers, had taken me to the theatre to see a performance of your play *Jeremiah*. You know, I've always asked myself whether I was inspired to become a rabbi by hearing Jeremiah's voice. You had put these words into your hero's mouth—and forgive me if I'm misquoting you here: 'He may not sleep who watches over the people. The Lord hath appointed me to watch and to give warning.' Isn't that the sort of leap of faith a rabbi makes?"

Other words spoken by the choirs in *Jeremiah* came flooding through Stefan's mind, words that he'd put in his characters' mouths more than thirty years earlier.

Wanderers, sufferers, our drink must be drawn from distant waters, evil their taste, bitter in the mouth, the nations will drive us from home after home, we will wander down suffering's endless roads, eternally vanquished, thralls at the hearths where in passing we rest.

How had he been able to write that in 1916?

Henrique Hemle, the chief rabbi of Rio, said he was originally from Hamburg. He had fled the Reich in 1935 along with his wife and two children. Hamburg, he contemplated, had no doubt been cleansed of all its Jews, maybe Hemle's family was dying of cold and hunger in the east, just like all of Berlin's and Vienna's Jews. Or maybe—as the BBC had reported on 30th November—Hemle's family had been among those five thousand German Jews executed at Kaunas in Lithuania as soon as they'd left the trains. Maybe Hemle's family had been lucky and been cooped up in the large ghetto in Minsk, previously occupied by Belarusian Jews, all of whom had been executed, down to the last one, in order to make room for those lucky German Jews. Stefan didn't ask after Hemle's family. It was the golden rule that everyone had abided by ever since the news had spread that Germany and Austria were in the process of becoming *judenrein*. Nobody asked questions any more. Everyone preferred to remain in the dark. They sought relief in ignorance and uncertainty. They knew. The families that had been driven out of the Reich had been expelled from the land of the living. They walked through the timeless woods, wandering, side by side, surrounded by anguished cries, hordes of fraternal spectres, all of whom were pale, naked and tormented, as they marched firm-footed and with dignity towards the darkness, doleful shadows walking in the freezing air, trembling in the fog, women leading the way as they held back their tears, watching their children vanish into the realm of endless pain, letting the fingers of their little loved ones slip out of their grasp, saying their goodbyes without opening their mouths, spilling torrents of silent, invisible tears, the endless grief of mothers looking on as reality unfolds to reveal an infinite grey expanse, an ocean of heaped-up bodies, the place of lovers' rendezvous and family reunions. The next world.

"I was very moved by your reply to my invitation," the rabbi continued, "to celebrate the day of Yom Kippur with us at the Great Synagogue in Rio. You apologized by saying that 'to your great shame', you did not have a religious upbringing. You shouldn't feel ashamed, Mr Zweig. That was the way things were done at the time. We were Germans first and foremost, Austrians first and foremost. In those times, we simply followed in our fathers' footsteps. Our fathers were great builders and soldiers for both the Second Reich and Hindenburg. It was our misfortune to place all our hopes in progress and emancipation rather than in God and our ancestors. You know, my father, who was an eminent professor at the University of Hamburg, one day confided in me that, like many others Jews at that time, he had been tempted to convert to Christianity. I inherited my faith from my grandfather, who taught me to read the Torah and to believe in God, go figure why religion seems to skip a generation… I'm not here to lecture but… you see yourself as far removed from your Jewish identity, and I'm aware of your fierce opposition to Zionism as you abhor all forms of nationalism. But let me tell you something, down in the depths of your soul there is something in you that is rooted to our Jewish traditions. Your *Jeremiah* is steeped in Jewish culture. What about Mendel the bookseller? Look at your friend and mentor Freud. Freud didn't hesitate in stripping us of our only heroes, and turned Moses into an Egyptian with his essay on monotheism, breaking our only idol at the same time that our synagogues were being burnt down. Even in your darkest hours you didn't commit such a sacrilege. You instead gave us an inkling of hope, brought our old epics to life with *The Buried Candelabrum*. I'm not that naive you know. I know that there isn't a single rabbi left alive in Germany, or for that matter in Poland and Ukraine. The Jewish world is being annihilated. In a year or maybe five, you and I, my dear Mr Zweig, may very well be among the last survivors of the tribe of Israel. That's why we need to fight—even if we're tempted to rejoin our loved ones, even if we feel ashamed that we're free to breathe while they are left gasping for air. The great Reich won't have a moment of peace so long as there is still a single rabbi left alive to read the Torah and wear his tefillin and tallith—even if that rabbi is ten thousand miles away from Berlin. They will want to come looking for him and will dispatch an entire army to do so. They claim that the Reich is slowing its advance through Russia in order to kill Jewish children—may God watch over those innocent souls. So imagine Goebbels finding out that Zweig is still alive and wielding the German tongue better than anyone... If you'll forgive this piece of advice, don't keep yourself inside this prison. According to our tradition, man defines himself first and foremost according to his relationships with others. We measure one life in the light of another. I'm not asking you to open yourself up to God, it is undoubtedly a bad moment to choose to put your faith in His hands given that He seems to have been increasingly turning His back on His people. Only allow me to speak to you as a rabbi, renew your relationships with people—there we have it, this is the reason behind my visit, please come and take part in the Passover Seder. The Pesach this year will have greater resonance than any Pesach before. This old story we're going to read on the night of the Seder, that story about the Pharaoh ordering the execution of all our firstborn sons, is the same tragedy our European martyrs are living today. Come and share our meal of bitter herbs and matzo bread and hear the Haggadah. Rabbi Akiva and Rabbi Eliezer will tell us the story of our wandering, bondage, misery and death. They will teach us that the darkest hour is just before the dawn. You and your wife need to hear those words. Come and pray, even if you aren't a believer. The sadness that afflicts us is too much for one man to bear, even if that man is the great Stefan Zweig… Well, there we have it, I won't inconvenience you any longer, but… promise me you'll try to make it."

He replied that he would do his best. He accompanied rabbi Hemle to the front steps. When it was time to close the door on him, he recalled some more words from his *Jeremiah*:

I have cursed my God and extinguished Him from my soul.

*

Above Petrópolis, the sky was no longer a bright azure. It was the middle of the tropical summer and a swarm of black clouds had unleashed a heavy rainfall. It felt as if they were breathing water. It no longer resembled anything like Baden and Sommerdigen. The air didn't smell sweet any more, the days were clammy and stultifying, while the nights were like being inside a furnace. Lotte spent most of her time gasping for air, going from the bed to the veranda, then opening and shutting the window, oppressed by the lack of air. She refrained from leaving the house lest she get caught in the rain, and whenever she surmounted her fears, she found herself smarting under the brunt of the storms. She would linger in the middle of the deserted street, as if paralysed, churning over the thought that just like trees attract lightning, she was a magnet for unhappiness. She felt cursed, punished for her errors, she had sinned in London, she had got involved with a married man and stolen him away from his wife and the Lord was now unleashing His wrath on her. She had sinned, she had fled from the war, tempted to cheat her destiny, abandoned her nearest and dearest to their unhappiness. She hadn't shared the bread of suffering with them. O the almighty Lord who turned ungodly women into statues of salt. Petrified, she lingered under the storm. She had entered into a covenant with this man, and this same man was afraid of everything except God's wrath. She had turned her back on her people while her loved ones tried to keep one another warm with their bodies in the freezing Polish cold—and there she was, with no one to hold her hand, having accompanied a man who sought escape and exile, seeking the peaceful bliss of enchanting dawns. The Lord is the only refuge, the Lord who blessed our forefathers, Abraham, Isaac and Jacob, the Lord who shielded us from tyrants and the revenge of oppressors, the Lord who helped those who believed in Him. Her sin was too great and the transgression unforgivable. Anguished and exhausted, she went back into the house. She swore she would never again brave the elements. Over the course of the following days, she meandered around the house, haggard and with lacklustre eyes, running short of breath at the slightest effort, uncommunicative, not daring to add to her unhappiness, letting her body speak for her instead, expressing herself with coughing fits. The physician was summoned at all hours of day and night. The pills had stopped working. He injected her with a drug he'd concocted himself and which he said would heal her. He looked for a vein and pricked her flesh in vain again and again, tightening the tourniquet. Her veins continually slipped from under his fingers, running away from the needle, and, having reached the end of his tether, the doctor, contrary to all logic, injected the solution into her anyway. Instead of coursing through her veins, the drug collected into a burning cyst on her arm. The doctor left on a reassuring note, the drug was now in her body, wasn't that what mattered in the end?

On occasion, she felt like her lungs were wholly devoid of air. She would worry that she would die of asphyxiation and feel herself being dragged into an abyss. Sometimes she could distinguish words of reassurance through her confusion. Her brain and blood were starved of oxygen and her body oppressed by pain. Her mind had lost all grip on reality.

Sometimes, while she lay at the bottom of the dark lake of suffering, she felt on the verge of deliverance. Liberated from the burden of her body, she would experience a sort of euphoria. Alas, every time she woke up, she was back in her body. She would get back on her feet, recover the use of her limbs and be able to see colours once more. She would reacquire sensation in her fingertips—and the man by her bedside would smile at her.

*

That morning, they had received another threatening letter, the third in ten days. "We've found you. We're going to kill you and that Jewish bitch of yours." Those words plunged him into fear. He knew that Rio was a veritable nest of German spies. The hotels were teeming with Gestapo agents. A few days earlier, the newspapers had run a story about the murder of an exile. Arthur Wolfe, a member of the old German Communist Party, had been found on the quay with a bullet in his head. Photographs of the body had made the front page.

The names of high-profile exiles had been disclosed. The morning papers had confirmed that he was on that list. Would he be next? They had managed to find him on the other side of the world. It seemed Petrópolis wasn't far enough removed from Berlin. Where could he possibly go? Should he disappear into the jungle and go to live with Amazonian tribes? Would Hitler determine his fate until the end of time?

Someone in town must have spotted him and divulged his address. He distrusted everyone. Everywhere he looked he saw informers skulking around each street corner. The baker's "Good morning" had a certain pointedness to it, the greengrocer had sold him rotten guavas, a new employee at the post office had insisted on being given his full address, the housekeeper's brother had been spotted near the house on the pretext of having come to see his sister, the woman who worked at the library had asked him why his books were no longer being published in German, while the waitress who worked at the Café Élégant never looked him in the eye. Was he being watched? One day he'd had the feeling he was being observed. On another occasion, he'd heard the sound of footsteps behind him throughout his walk. He had stopped walking and the sound of footsteps had also stopped. He hadn't turned around. What would he have seen if he had? A local or a blond giant in a trench coat and leather hat? He pictured himself making the headlines:

"Author of *Brazil, Land of the Future* killed."

He imagined the photo that would accompany the article. The sight of his corpse haunted him.

So long as he was in the house, he feared nothing. He always carried a vial of barbitone on his person. They would never catch him alive. They would never mutilate his body. He refused to bestow a picture of his bloodied face to posterity. The barbitone would work fast, before the assassins would have the chance to aim their guns, before they'd hear the door creak. Barbitone

LAURENT SEKSIK

was the ace up their sleeve. It was their last line of defence. Walter Benjamin had had his vial, as had Ernst Weiss and Erwin Rieger—and countless others, all his Viennese cousins and his friends in Berlin, people whose last wish had been not to fall into the hands of the Nazis, and who had sought a farcical victory over the forces of barbarism. All the exiles whispered in hushed tones about this friendly vial, their fellow sufferer, their exit visa. The last journey.

*

Stefan had long hesitated paying a visit to Bernanos, who was now living in Barbacena, a few hours' train ride from Petrópolis. He had wanted to spare the Frenchman his inconsolable grief and heavy silences, in other words, his presence. Yet he wanted to see a writer, to reawaken the feeling of sharing life with a kindred soul—to meet with another author who had opted for life in exile. He longed to be able to speak French once again, to discover a corner of Paris deep in the heart of the Brazilian jungle. Who knew? Perhaps his host's enthusiasm would prove infectious and he would finally find the strength to start writing again.

Bernanos had taken a path parallel to his own, and like Stefan, he had left Europe, despairing of all those who'd given way to Hitlerism, and had been lured away by the allure of Latin America. The Frenchman had pushed even farther into the country, winding up in a desolate region of barren hills three hundred kilometres to the north of Rio, a place called Cruz das Almas. Aside from a shared passion for Brazil, Stefan and Bernanos were equally fascinated by the Fall, the longing for a paradise lost—for Stefan it was *fin de siècle*, cosmopolitan Vienna, while for Bernanos it was the old Christian France. They also bonded over their

110

abhorrence of fascism and communism. As far as literature was concerned, the chronicler of human passions felt a kinship with the "prophet of the sacred". Just like Bernanos, Stefan considered Balzac's *The Human Comedy* as the most successful work of literature ever composed and saw Dostoevsky as an undisputed master. He had read Bernanos's *Under the Sun of Satan* and *Diary of a Country Priest*. He had adored the fiery urgency of his scenes, his fragmentary aesthetic, how those books grew increasingly insular until they opened onto vast abysses. Bernanos's characters were all a little unhinged, full of a sense of their own heroism. Then there was their cosmic dimension. Stefan admired the manner in which his host explored the notion of despair. Nevertheless, he feared meeting Bernanos as much as he desired it. It wasn't the author's anti-Semitic past that frightened him. Bernanos's fight against Franco, his immediate denunciation of the Vichy regime—and Stefan's reading of *A Diary of My Times*—had allowed him to forget all about *Right-Thinking People's Greatest Fear*. He didn't know whether or not people had the capacity to change, but he was willing to give this devout Catholic the benefit of the doubt. Redemption by way of exile. After all, Bernanos had a long track record of making a break with the past. He'd broken off all ties with Action Française, Maurras and the Vatican. He might very well have rid himself of his hatred of Jews. Bernanos's fiercely anti-Semitic past was of little import. Something else held Stefan back, and made him postpone the date of his visit week after week. First of all, there was Bernanos's unwavering love of the motherland, and his quasi-mystical belief in God. Stefan abhorred nationalism and did not believe in God—neither the Jewish God nor the Christian one. He no longer held out any hope for man and feared the excesses prompted by political convictions. Every time Stefan had taken part in anti-Nazi demonstrations, he had done so half-heartedly. Although it was a difficult stance to defend, he believed that Jews shouldn't concern themselves with anti-Semitism, which only brought dishonour on people who subscribed to that idea. Stefan hadn't done anything wrong and didn't need to defend himself. He only cared about one thing: to safeguard his freedom. Alas, these days his inner world was a heap of ruins.

Physically exhausted and on the verge of a nervous breakdown, Stefan feared a confrontation with Bernanos, a highly opinionated man who was prone to flights of anger. Stefan dreaded being flattened under Bernanos's rock of faith. He didn't want to justify his pessimism, defeatism and weaknesses in front of the French national bard and Christ's Messenger. Although he didn't want to admit it to himself, he was also afraid that Bernanos might read his mind and glimpse into the recesses of his soul, just like his hero, the Abbé Donissan. That he would only have to look at him to discern the "black disease" that was gnawing at him, his cowardly actions, or, worse still, that he might even look upon him with pity.

Nevertheless, one day he forgot about all his apprehensions. He wanted to talk literature with an actual writer—when journalists like Feder and editors like Koogan spoke about literature they only really talked about books. When Lotte suggested they go to Cruz das Almas, he consented, especially after she had assured him they would take come back the same evening.

The farther they left Petrópolis behind, the more the landscape shed its colours, revealing a post-apocalyptic terrain with endless peaks and parched valleys. After an hour in that lethargic train compartment, Stefan already regretted his decision. Why did he feel like he was a student undergoing a process of self-examination in front of a professor of moral theology?

The trip seemed to last for ever. Once they'd arrived, he got up, bone-tired, stepped out of the compartment and examined his reflection in a mirror. He was tempted to jump on the next train and go home. However, he was met by a man on the platform who claimed he had been sent by Bernanos and who led them to a car. After a half-hour drive through a desolate landscape, they entered a forest and found themselves on a deserted road. Bernanos was waiting for them at the end of it, holding the reins of a horse. The car came to a stop. Stefan got out. Bernanos embraced him as though they'd been old friends — they had never crossed paths hitherto—and kissed Lotte's hand. They then crossed a field and stepped inside a rather austere stone house.

"Welcome to my palace," Bernanos said, smiling. Some children came to greet the guests, then quickly ran outside. Bernanos's wife suggested some refreshments and brought biscuits and fruit. They sat down. They drank. Stefan forced himself to answer the questions regarding his life in Brazil enthusiastically. He asked after his host's writing projects and tried to keep up with the latter's zest. There were awkward silences. Bernanos stood up and headed over to the wireless on the table, which a friend from Syria had recently dropped off on one of his visits. Bernanos enthused about being finally able to hear news from around the world, and suggested they tune in to the daily bulletin. His suggestion elicited no response.

They swapped stories about other writers living in exile. Jules Romains was in Mexico, Roger Caillois was in Buenos Aires, while all the rest lived in New York. Caillois had offered Bernanos an opinion column in the pages of *Les Lettres françaises*.

"You would do well to write for them too... an article penned by you would be highly prized. A dispatch by Stefan Zweig from South America, where you're admired and celebrated, would be like a message in a bottle that would wash ashore in France, where you're also widely loved, that would be something!"

Stefan didn't want to hear about politics, nor about writing appeals to South Americans asking them to join the war effort. He was only interested in one thing. Roger Martin du Gard had confided in him that Bernanos was prone to fits of despair. He would have loved to question his host on the veracity of these allegations. Could it be that such a giant might also suffer from pangs of solitude and the privations of exile? But he gave up on the idea of broaching the subject: the man in front of him seemed to him to sleep the sleep of the just.

"I know," Bernanos carried on, "that you're a humble man and that you wish to ignore just how widely influential you are. Plus, we feel so far removed from everything here, where sadness constantly hangs over our heads and saps our strength. But we must find the courage to react. One must have faith, and I'm not talking about having faith in a god—in fact being an atheist seems far more rational to me than believing in God as an engineer. No, we must have faith in our inner strength and our purpose. As writers and vagabonds we possess a most formidable weapon. We must prove ourselves worthy of this gift for writing, worthy of this divine bless-ing. Your pen and your name constitute a formidable sword that can smite all the Goebbelses and Lavals, as well as all those other cowards and idiots. Preach and practise what you preach. The columns of the *Jornal* and *Correio da Manhã* are ripe for the taking, as are the hearts and minds of all Brazilians. Join me. It's now or never. All will be decided today. As we speak, the International Union of American Republics is meeting at a summit. Its lead-ers are going to choose which side they're on. You know as well as I do that President Vargas has been on the fence and that at one point he preferred Mussolini to Roosevelt. It was a close call and we have Minister Aranha to thank for that. The leaders of other South American countries haven't yet broken off ties with Germany. Imagine if they decided to align themselves with the Axis Powers. That would be the end of all our hopes. Write then and throw your hat into the ring. An article bearing your name might help sway public opinion and touch the hearts of people in Argentina and Uruguay. You're a real moral authority. I know how highly you value your freedom. We both detest partisan hacks. We don't serve the interests of any ideologies. Above all, try not to see me as an evangelist or a soldier for Action Française. I'm a just a simple cattleman, but like you I remain a stalwart defender of liberty. This gift that weighs so heavily on our shoulders and is such a source of happiness can sometimes overwhelm us since it comes with responsibilities. We are missionaries. All those do-gooders and right-thinkers have turned the writer's mission into a joke. Must we really remain above the fray? I was right in the thick of the fray in 1914 and the fight I'm proposing now pales in comparison. This struggle is about hanging on to hope, to our purpose, to pride, to courage, this fight will warm our hearts. There's no worse torture than boredom and despair. The world we hold dear will be saved by writers and poets. Ever since Munich, democratically elected leaders have been skirting around the issue in fear. Fear is the Devil's work. We who live on the other side of the world can no longer stand on the sidelines. Needless to say, we can't defeat the Devil on our own. Yet if we don't take a heroic stand, we'll never be able to live with ourselves… please don't misunderstand me, I don't say all this lightly, it wasn't easy for me to lend my pen to the cause of the Free French. I'm no pamphleteer. God knows how much it's grieved me to be unable to write novels. Yet, between you and me, is it even possible to write novels in dark days such as these? Does the light that illuminated our works still survive in our hearts? No, this isn't a time for fiction. So long as there are enough of us and if we show ourselves resolved to continue the struggle, Marshal Pétain's France will be a thing of the past and Clemenceau will come back. The Seine will run red with the blood of traitors. For the moment, alas, the Nazis are marching up and down the quays of Paris while idiots line up to cheer them on. This is the sort of clamour we have to pierce through in order to make ourselves heard. We are novelists walking through the shadows guided only by our instincts. We must emerge out of this darkness with clean consciences. United we stand, divided we fall. The world needs to hear your voice, my dear friend."

Stefan was reluctant to answer, to argue, to hurt his host's feelings, to defend the indefensible. It would undoubtedly be wise to say, "Yes Mr Bernanos, you're right, we're all in the same boat, all men are possessed with steely resolve and a rebel soul, humanity is made up of heroes like you, all of whom are endowed with a free will, follow one faith, are indestructible demigods fighting the forces of evil with flowers rather than guns." Yet he couldn't say these things out loud. Before he even knew what had happened, he'd felt his lips move and had thanked his host for his words and said that he felt supremely honoured to have heard them. But Bernanos was wrong. Nobody in the world, not even in this distant corner of it, needed to hear Stefan Zweig's words, nor read any of his writing. Besides, would people really be able to hear his words above the din of battle? How would his quavering, plaintive voice fare against the Führer's roaring rants and Goebbels's howls? Or his blubbering versus the shrill cries of Stukas or the barking of dogs? How loud would his voice be when he dragged it out of the dark well of despair? It would be lost to the wind. How could Bernanos possibly expect it would reach the shores of Europe? One word from him and the gates of hell would be thrown open? And what did he have to say anyway, what was his message? He was sorry to come across as a coward, but he hadn't changed his mind in thirty years; he had stayed true to Romain Rolland's call to pacifism in 1914. He would remain "above the fray", even if Rolland himself had since rescinded his pacifism. Rolland would for ever remain a sage, a beacon of Enlightenment. As he spoke, he recalled a few remarks Rolland had made in his letter to him: "I don't see you settling down in Brazil. It's far too late in our lives to put down roots again, and without any roots, we'll turn into shadows."

Stefan felt like a shadow. He no longer had the strength to make himself heard. He'd travelled too much, wandered too much, suffered too many delusions, too many regrets, too many bouts of nostalgia. He had shared all he'd known, and written down all the little white lies that he'd cooked up in his dreams. He thought the well of eternal truths in his soul had dried up and that no stone had been left unturned. What was more—and Bernanos knew this well—he'd never had a warrior's temperament. The Mitteleuropa Stefan had written about had been a place of poets, dreamers, an enchanted world, a children's fairy tale. The pages of history that were being written today described a black wedding. Picking a fight with the Devil? He was too old for that, he lacked both the strength and the determination. The slightest breeze knocked him over and they expected him to stand up to Hitler's armies! The SS soldiers would double over in laughter faced with an enemy like him. His despair had burnt the bridge connecting him to the world of men. He was washed up, he no longer believed in anything. He envied his host's inexhaustible energy as much as he envied Jules Romains's fighting spirit. Humanity needed men like them. But what could they possibly need him for? He was nothing but deadweight. Perhaps that was why everything he'd ever loved and stood for had been blown away. He was destined to disappear and that was for the best. Maybe this was the price he had to pay for victory? There would be no place for him in the new world that would arise from the ruins of the present. He no longer found pleasure in writing, nor did he engage in conversation with enthusiasm. Making his voice heard? All he wanted was silence.

Bernanos made no reply. Lotte stepped in to fill the silence the conversation had left in its wake. She asked whether life had been harsh in those untamed lands. They spoke about raising horses and planting manioc. After a long time, Stefan broke his silence. He asked Lotte what time they needed to catch the train home. He was tired. He wanted to be back home before it got too late.

*

The train inched forwards in the blackness of the night. Stefan hadn't managed to rid himself of the anger that his meeting with Bernanos had plunged him in. He had thought visiting him would fire him up and act as a soothing balm. Yet the opposite result had been achieved. Bernanos had lectured him and he'd had to defend himself. He was his own worst advocate. Once again, he had expressed only a fraction of his thoughts. Truth be told, his work had always been fuelled by defeatism rather than pacifism. As far as he was concerned, the defeated were sublime beings who occupied a moral high ground. The humiliated were superior to the master race. How could he get that message across? People expected him to speak like a liberator from glorious heights—General Zweig, commander in chief of the vanquished, the ragged, the annihilated, as they marched towards death, advancing in serried ranks, silently, dumbstruck by the sheer scale of the efforts that had been made to wipe them

118

out; the commander of a pious race, petrified in the face of end-less barbarism, a race that had been wrung from the plains of Poland and captured on the spot—a child lifting its eyes towards a man in black filled with absolute hatred who aimed his rifle in his direction, a mother stunned by the unprecedented horrors unrolling before her eyes, old men stumbling in the cold, whole families mown down by machine-gun fire. General Zweig at the head of the army of the dead, is that what Bernanos wanted? He thought about his first published short story, "In the Snow", which he'd published in 1901 at the age of twenty in Theodor Herzl's *Die Welt*. Yes, although he hated nationalism in all its guises, he had published his first story in a Zionist newspaper. He had always preferred the tragic destiny of Jews in exile over the proud destiny that the tribe of Israel had been promised once they'd returned to their ancestral land. What had he written in that first novella, which had been published over forty years ago, back at the beginning of that promising century, drunk on the promise of a glorious tomorrow? What had he written in 1900 when everyone else his age had been busy writing love poems? "In the Snow"! The story of a ghetto on the outskirts of a German town close to the Polish border during the Middle Ages. A poor, isolated Jewish community, an inward-looking community that devoutly worshipped its God, terrified by the thought that the world around them might overhear their prayers. Finally, one night, a messenger arrives with frightening news: the "Flagellants" were coming, wave after wave of them advancing towards the ghetto in serried ranks, drunk on hate and baying for Jewish blood. Having ransacked the countryside, the Flagellants, who were to Germany what Cossacks were to Russia, had pillaged the surrounding shtetls, wiping out its inhabitants. Yes, he had been only twenty years old—the finest age to be—and he had written it at the beginning of a century that promised to be even brighter than the age of Enlightenment, the most liberating century of all time. As happy as a German Jew could be. The young Stefan had gone back to the fourteenth century, the time of the Flagellants, the time of rural horrors, the time of small massacres, the time of the Black Death, the time before the pogroms; he retraced his little Jewish community's origins, and where did he lead it as it fled the advancing German hordes? He followed them into Poland, yes, he followed those poor wretches as they pushed their sleighs through the Polish plains while being hunted down by the German hordes. And what had the young Stefan, who was now a toothless old coward, heard? He'd heard the sobbing of those distraught women, the children's persistent cries, the roaring of a storm brooding on the horizon, the cacophony of moans and anguished howls. What had the young ambitious Stefan, who dreamt of literary glories and transient loves, seen? He had seen the snow thickly cover everything in that sharp cold, slowing the advance of the wagons and freezing both the horses and their masters. *And their fear of death turns to hopeless resignation.* Those had been the exact words he'd written as a twenty-year-old. The funeral song that the storm had hummed and the glacial cold that had annihilated the fugitives. The German Jews who had perished due to the cold on their way to the Polish paradise. *Josua holds his fiancée with cold hands. She is dead already, although he does not know it.*

The icy casket that was Poland. The biggest mass grave in the world. That had been his first published work, a twenty-year-old's bleak vision, the freezing winding sheet of Israel.

Lotte felt compelled to pull him out of his depression:

"Tell me one of your stories, it's very cold in this compartment, warm me up with one of your stories. I love it when you tell me one of your stories. Share an episode of your life with me, something you've never told anyone else."

Was that because the train had passed by a village where the cross on top of the church loomed high above the roofs of houses? His memory led him down a road towards a village in Alsace. The image of Gunsbach came back to him, as did that of a man whom he had once loved. His face lit up. In a clear voice, he began telling Lotte about his last meeting with Albert Schweitzer. It had taken place many years earlier—and how unforgettable it had been. After having visited the cathedral in Strasbourg, Stefan had boarded the train for Colmar with a couple of friends, then taken a bus in order to reach the village of Gunsbach. That was where the celebrated physician—who besides being a great humanist was also a renowned musicologist—had lived. Schweitzer, a virtuoso pianist, who had written a remarkable study on Bach, had told his guests he would play a few pieces for them. He'd had Gunsbach's church opened and had begun playing with his long, slender fingers on an organ that had been built according to his own specifications. The bars of one of the Advent Cantatas had resounded in the nave. It had been a moment of overwhelming peace. While Schweitzer's hands had played the keys, a divine presence had inhabited the chapel.

He paused and, suddenly excited, asked Lotte whether he'd ever told her about his meeting with Rodin in Paris in 1905. "No, no," she lied, "you've never told me that story, tell me all about it!" In the middle of the cold, dark night, Stefan told her that story, which she'd already heard him tell a hundred times before over various dinners; about when he'd been invited to the great sculptor's home when still a young man, and about the unbelievable spectacle he'd been privileged to witness. Forgetting his guest's presence, the genius had stood surrounded by his sculptures and had begun touching up the statue of a woman with a putty knife. After he'd told her about Rodin, he moved on to Jaurès, Rilke, Alma Mahler and Maurice Ravel. The more they travelled through the night, the more a light drew out entire swathes of Stefan's life from oblivion; and the closer they drew to dawn, the brighter Vienna shone. By the time the train had begun to slow down, Lotte, who was still listening enraptured, believed herself an oriental princess who was being told a thousand and one tales.

*

Around eight o'clock that evening, Feder came to pay them a visit. As usual, the Berliner had brought his host a book that he'd purchased for him in Rio. But Zweig no longer read any contemporary authors. He was taken up with rereading *The Human Comedy*, had resumed work on a German rendition of Homer, was in the middle of reading a selection of Shakespeare's plays and was leisurely rereading Goethe's *Wilhelm Meister*.

"Now I know the books you would take with you on a desert island," Feder observed.

They were already living on a desert island.

"Let us recap: Montaigne, Goethe, Homer, Shakespeare, Balzac. I can't see anything more to add to them. The Bible, maybe… Well, I've brought you the latest Thomas Mann, *Lotte in Weimar*."

This had been one of the last books that a British newspaper had commissioned Stefan to review. He had written to Mann to express his admiration and promised to send him the review once it had been published. Yet it had never come to pass. He had fled from London and had never written to Thomas Mann again. He was fed up with all those lies and sycophancy. He had been ashamed by all those words of praise in his piece. Truth be told, he had hated the Nobel laureate's novel, the account of Goethe's last meeting with Lotte, his childhood sweetheart, in Weimar, the same Lotte who served as inspiration for the heroine in *The Sorrows of Young Werther*. He had abhorred the manner in which Mann had treated his subject, its coldness, that descriptive exhaustiveness. The whole novel had read like the minutes of a boring meeting. In his own works, Zweig had always dismissed getting the facts straight, and had claimed the right to portray reality in a subjective way. He had never tried fully to define his subjects, or to place them within definitive boundaries. He wasn't a geologist. He was only interested in fragmentary perspectives. He saw himself as an Impressionist. What good would a certificate of authenticity amount to? First and foremost, he was interested in the emotional impulses that made his characters tick. He knew that one couldn't reduce a man to the visible facts of his life. On the contrary, one had to employ one's elective affinities with one's subject in order to establish an intimate bond, to deal in shades of grey rather than in revealed truths.

"It's funny to notice how the choices you made as a writer reveal your true inner nature. Mann opted to write about Goethe, while you chose to focus on Kleist and Nietzsche. You look for a path through the darkness and wander from country to country, with neither children nor a fixed address, and now you've buried yourself away in this godforsaken place in the middle of nowhere. Meanwhile, Mann proceeds full steam ahead. Mann surrounds himself with people and protects himself. He has placed himself at the crossroads so as to watch all comings and goings, he's the sun around which everyone else revolves. Whereas you have escaped to a place where nothing happens and have reached a point of no return. Mann is planning his reconquest of the literary world.

LAURENT SEKSIK

Mann is busy building a statue to himself, while concealing his true nature. Mann will never own up to his pederastic inclinations. Mann conceals anything that might compromise his public image. Mann sees himself as peerless. Mann looks for light and finds it in Thomas Mann. On the other hand, here you are doing your utmost to disappear."

How could he help being drawn to Kleist instead of Goethe, since he had always been more drawn to losers rather than winners? He nursed an unbounded admiration for poets who'd met tragic ends. He had dedicated *The Struggle with the Daemon*, his finest collection of essays, to poets such as these. His mind found itself in perfect harmony with those mad souls. He found himself gripped by the same torments that plagued Nietzsche and Hölderlin.

Well before he had gone into exile, before the First World War had even broken out, indeed as far back as his memory reached, his dark thoughts had always been the breeding ground for all his ideas. He had never felt at ease in the world. Every time he thought about his childhood, he remembered seeing a shadow hovering above his head. As the years had gone by, this shadow had stretched. It now covered the entirety of the sky. Alas, he could truly claim one of Kleist's phrases as his own: "My heart is so sore, that I might almost say the daylight hurts my nose whenever I stick it out of the window."

"May I ask you a question," Feder asked, "...even though it's indiscreet? Well... in your essay on Kleist, you talk about his death, about his double suicide with Henriette Vogel, his second wife, in... in quite a strange way."

He pretended not to have understood the question.

"Yes," Feder pressed, "your words are suffused with empathy, as if you were fascinated by his suicide, you give the impression

124

that you agree with his decision to kill himself. If my memory serves me well, you even add that he was the greatest German poet of all time because his death had been the most beautiful. You sublimate his horrible death."

Feder saw Zweig's tired black eyes land on him, full of pain and bitterness. He looked like a deer caught in the headlights. Feder was both frightened by that look and filled with endless compassion.

"Please reassure me that when you wrote that his suicide had been a masterpiece it was merely a flourish?"

Of course! That had been nothing but a figure of speech. He had wanted to bring the conversation to an end and went to fix himself a drink.

Yes, he had written all those foolish, dangerous sentences—and many others still—about how sublime that suicide had been. Yes, he admired how grandiose Kleist's decision had been, and yes, he believed it placed Kleist above all others. After having shot his wife in the heart, the poet had turned the gun on himself and fired a bullet into his brain. Yes, his *Kleist* had dared to praise that deadly deed! He had written those lines in 1925, when pack hounds had yet to start snapping at his heels and long before death had become Germany's motto. Back then, peace had reigned over Europe, although the continent was already headed towards the edge of the precipice.

"Forgive me for raising the matter again," Feder persevered, hesitating more than ever, "but... has Lotte... never read your *Kleist?*"

Feder lowered his gaze to the floor, knowing he had crossed the line with that question. Yet he couldn't stop himself from adding:

"I say that... because of... the coincidences."

What was Feder driving at? Of course, he had described in great detail how the poet had put an end to his life after having killed his second wife. True, he had spoken of it as a heroic act, as the most affectionate act ever committed between two lovers. The suicide had undoubtedly inspired some of the finest passages in that book. But what was Feder accusing him of? What coincidences had he spotted? That Kleist had left his first wife, Marie, and chosen a younger woman, an invalid, as his last companion? The question was pointless, absurd even. Feder was looking for coincidences whereas it had all been a simple twist of fate. Or maybe he thought that Zweig was a psychic, who had been able to divine his own destiny by retracing that of his heroes? Or maybe that Zweig believed he was Kleist? Or that he would shoot his wife in the heart the following day? Is that what he was driving at? Feder began apologizing profusely. His host carried on. No, Lotte had never read his *Kleist*, she'd never thumbed through *The Struggle with the Daemon*. But so that he might not read any malice into this, Lotte also hadn't read his play *The Lamb of the Poor Man*, or even his *Fouché* or his *Magellan*. He wasn't going to force his wife to read all of his works! Yet if she ever would read that book, he didn't think she would be offended. Lotte was an innocent soul. She didn't go looking for evil where there was none to be found.

In the adjacent room, Lotte was eavesdropping on the conversation with her ear glued to the wall, horrified. Stefan was lying through his teeth, and, worse still, he had lied to her, his wife, his devoted wife, she who could understand everything, she who had seen everything, who had endured everything. She thought back to the advice he'd given her, whose meaning she hadn't grasped at the time. When she'd opened up his *Kleist* to read it, he'd told her, "Oh, that's hardly worth reading, the book isn't worth much, one day when you will have read all of my other essays and biographies, then it might be worth your while to read that… that is, maybe…" In her naivety, she had believed him. Why did she have to take orders from him?

Then, all of a sudden, her hatred turned in on herself. She forgave him all his lies. It was her fault if he hadn't deemed her worthy of his confidences, if he hadn't judged her brave enough to confront the secrets hidden between that book's lines. Was his opinion of her so low that he would go to the lengths of sparing her the reading of that book? Had she shown him a side of herself that looked frightened of everything? He clearly couldn't trust her. Yes, she was the guilty party, she had shown herself too fragile when he'd needed someone strong by his side. Oh, how much he must have missed Friderike! Now she had to show him a reckless side of her, once, only once, so that he might look upon her as he'd never seen her! She dried her tears, stopped in front of the mirror, fixed her hair and took a deep, determined breath. She opened the bedroom door and walked resolutely down the corridor to the lounge, going right up to Feder and giving him a firm handshake, before throwing her husband a sharp look—and reading a surprised look in his eyes. She turned around, headed towards the library, leant on one of the shelves, reached out with a steady hand towards the volume in question, pulled it out and slowly—as if stunned that a bolt of lightning hadn't struck her down—headed back into the bedroom.

She experienced a surge of pride. She had finally shown herself determined, ready to brave the storm, an intrepid woman, and now saw herself in a new light. She had found a new sense of self-confidence. Following that act of bravery, he would love her more than ever before. He would never lie to her again.

She sat down on the bed, swaying with happiness and euphoria.

Sitting up straight, she began reading the book. From the very first lines, she experienced a profound sadness at discovering that Stefan had used his portrait of Kleist to talk about himself, "the eternal vagabond on the run".

As early as page 9, she was already on the brink of tears:

…left Marie von Kleist, who was also dear to him, in loneliness and neglect; and dragged Henriette Vogel down with him to death… he retired more and more into himself, growing more solitary even than nature had created him.

She spilt her first tears when she read:

Like every other of his hyperbolical affects, Kleist's passion for a fellowship on which a joint suicide could alone put the seal remained a mystery to his friends. Vainly did he seek a companion into the Valley of the Shadow. One and all they contemptuously or shudderingly rejected the proposal.

Then she was grief-stricken by the following:

He encountered a woman, hitherto almost a stranger, who thanked him for his strange invitation. She was an invalid, whose death could not in any case be long delayed, for her body was inwardly devoured by cancer even as Kleist's mind was devoured by weariness of life. Though herself incapable of forming a vigorous resolution, she was sensitive and highly suggestible, and therefore open to the promptings of his morbid enthusiasm; she agreed to plunge with him into the unknown.

The "coincidences" that Feder had mentioned reverberated in her mind. She carried on reading:

> At bottom this somewhat priggish and sentimental wife of a tax-collector was of a type uncongenial to Kleist... She who would have been too petty, too soft, too weak for him as a living companion, was welcomed by him as a comrade in death.

Her vision started to blur at the sight of these sentences:

> Although another woman swore to be his companion in death, his thoughts turned to her for whom he had lived and whom he loved, to Marie von Kleist.

The name "Friderike Marie Zweig" resounded in her mind, and then came the terrible end:

> In the high spirits of honeymooners, the couple drive to the Wannsee. The host at the inn hears them laughing, sees them sporting merrily in the fields, can tell how they drank their coffee with gusto in the open air. Then, at the prearranged hour, came the two pistol shots, in swift succession, the first that with which Kleist pierced his companion's heart, the second that with which (barrel in mouth) he blew out his own brains. His hand did not falter. It was true that he knew better how to die than to live.

She tried to pull herself together. No, he wasn't a psychic. There was no way he could have foreseen his own end fifteen years ago. That panegyric to suicide was nothing but a work of literature.

She leafed through the book and stopped when she came across Kleist's last poem, which her husband praised as his finest.

> You beam through the blindfold covering my eyes
> At me with the radiance of a thousand suns.
> Wings have put forth on both my shoulders,
> My spirit lifts through the ether's silent spaces.

The lines of the poem he'd written for his sixtieth birthday came flooding back to her:

> Presentiments of closing day,
> When our desires are gone,
> Soothe us far more than they dismay
> Now, in the setting sun…

> The world before us never lay
> So fair, or life so true,
> As in the glow of parting day,
> When shadows dim the view.

They were written in the same vein, and even sounded the same; "coincidences" indeed, as Feder had put it. All her feelings of anger suddenly abandoned her. She no longer resented him for lying to her, and she no longer felt any jealousy towards Friderike. She stretched out on the bed, staring into space. He was her first and only love. If he has chosen to model himself after Kleist, then I will be Kleist's wife, I will be his last companion, I will go with him towards the light. I will grasp his hand in the pitch black. I will precede him to where destiny sees fit to take us, towards the unknown place that fate has set aside for us. So much the worse if that road only takes us past gloomy shores devoid of all life, where it's difficult to breathe. I know how much it hurts when it's difficult to breathe. It's been a long time now since my lungs were broken beyond repair and my body is nothing but an open wound. Each breath that filters all the way down to my bronchi tastes as bitter as though it were my last. I know the scent of death as it lurks in the wings. Death hangs over me night and day, it sniffs up all my air and breathes it in. I am both familiar with it and haunted by it. I'm not afraid of death. My inner voice isn't pleading for its life and I'm not held back by any regrets. The life I have led and the future that lies before me exude a poisoned air. My last hour will bring me merciful relief. Life has turned me into a weak, pitiful person, contemptible too, the silent woman, isn't that what they call me? My whole life has been a struggle. I have tasted bitterness, solitude and misfortune, I have never been loved. I will walk with him through the darkness. And if everything is ice cold in the middle of the forest, the fire that burns deep within me will keep us warm. My boundless enthusiasm will warm his soul. My tears will console his pain and sorrow. His heart will be inaccessible in the next life, but my love knows no confines and it will reach his heart, my love will be so strong that it will carry his mortal remains. My love will reign in the kingdom of shadows. The next world will undoubtedly be too dark for him to see my real face, but the next sky will be studded with stars where I will be able to shine, where my pale spectre will exert its charms. Yes, in the next life we will taste unimaginable sweetness. So much the worse if I couldn't be his wife in this world. That is, if any woman could ever truly occupy such a place. I, Lotte Altmann, will be his companion for ever.

FEBRUARY

Monday, 16th February, in the evening.

T ORCHES HELD ALOFT by swarms of people were lighting
up the night in Rio. A rush of humanity came pouring out
of every street corner, winding down the hills, rolling out like a
tide, wave after wave, bursting out of crowded trams, spilling out
of the *favelas*, crowds of men, women and children dancing on
the pavements. It was a joyous masquerade, with people wearing
wigs, fake noses, their faces painted in bright colours, dressed
up like lords, devils, clowns, transvestites with quirky hats, top
hats, feather headdresses and fake tiaras. A cacophony of cries,
stamping, songs, drumming, maracas and trumpets rose from the
asphalt. The wind was shaking curtains, lanterns and garlands
on the balconies of buildings. Sung by thousands of mouths, the
sound of samba music filled the entire city, a loud pagan chant
that rose from the depths of time. The streets were overflowing
with life like a river in spate.

They walked in the middle of the crowds. They marched
ahead, gripped by the feverish atmosphere, gripped by a feeling
of euphoria. They had allowed themselves to be persuaded to

leave their sanctuary behind for three days in order to attend carnival, and were now being carried along by the crowds, away from the place of their distress. Drowning in the procession, they slipped into oblivion.

They had left Petrópolis a few hours earlier, a town so steeped in silence and bad dreams that it already seemed to them like a distant planet. As for Vienna, it seemed like a lifetime ago! Germany was a dead star. They could no longer hear the sound of funeral processions. In the midst of those delightful, restless crowds, they recovered their sight. Perhaps they were already dead and their ghosts were drifting through that bacchanalia? Tomorrow it would be Mardi Gras, while the following day would be Ash Wednesday. Time no longer followed the ancient order of days. They allowed themselves to be swallowed by that deafening crowd that swelled with boundless love. On the other side of the world, the earth was a dank dungeon where a mute people trudged through the snow. Here, on the other hand, the singing and dancing had filled their gloomy souls with light.

The crowd gave way to make room for a movable float. A single man in the middle of the street led the way, dancing a sarabande. Behind him was a horde of women in low-cut dresses, with heavy-set, voluptuous bodies, but whose feet seemed to be barely touching the ground. Farther behind was the first float, the flagship, which crawled along with a huge emblem emblazoned on its prow, and was accompanied by an orchestra. A man dressed like a master of ceremonies followed suit, followed hot on his heels by hundreds of dancers, beating time and moving forwards in a dispersed fashion. Then there came a succession of women and children in traditional Bahian dress, followed by more movable floats, topped with sculptures, gigantic guitars, statues of young men, two-headed monsters and idols, all overflowing with half-naked dancers. They clung to each other's hands so as not to be swept away by the crowd. They looked on, astonished by the sight of so much beauty and whimsy.

He wore a white suit and a panama hat. When he'd examined himself in the mirror of the room that his friend de Souza had put them up in, that vision of himself—as if dredged from a distant past—had made him smile. Lotte had emerged from the bathroom wearing a short, figure-hugging red dress, which left her back bare and which he'd never seen her wear before. She looked radiant and he had drawn close to her, kissed her lips and slid a hand over her shoulders. Then they had left, waiting on the front steps of the house for their host, as well as the Feders and the Koogan family to join them. Once they were all accounted for, they had headed off into the streets.

Overwhelmed by the crowds, they were led down the Avenida Central right up to the Praça Onze, a square deep in the heart of the black quarter, close to the Morro da Favela and the neighbourhoods of the Zona Norte. This was where nearly all *cariocas* seemed to have converged, singing a spellbinding, melancholic song to the tune of a samba. Koogan explained that the song, "Adeus, Praça Onze", evoked the sadness of the people at the forthcoming demolition of the Avenida Praça to make way for the future Avenida Presidente Vargas. Koogan wagered that "Adeus, Praça Onze" would be voted the most popular song of the 1942 carnival. Koogan admitted to a preference for "Saudade da Amélia", a song that belonged to a different musical genre and was more sentimental and melodious. Stefan asked him why any of this even mattered.

"You see," Koogan had replied, "this carnival is a little like our Bayreuth Festival."

Stefan had forgotten all about Bayreuth.

The air reverberated with the lyrics being chanted by the whole crowd.

"*Vão acabar com a Praça Onze, Não vai haver mais Escola de Samba, não vai Chora o tambourim, Chora o morro inteiro…*"

Koogan shouted the translation into Stefan's ear.

"They're going to tear down Praça Onze, there will be more samba, the tambourines will cry, the whole world is going to cry…"

The crowd was on the move again—a shapeless stream that undulated under a hail of confetti and ticker tape. In the midst of that gigantic, joyful fray, Stefan was seized by a sudden panic. He had lost hold of Lotte's hand. He looked around frantically. The thought that she might have drowned in that human flood terrified him. Pushing his way through the pandemonium, he began screaming out her name, a cry that was lost in the midst of that racket. Everyone around him was lost in jubilation. A man wearing a skeleton costume and a skull mask roared in his face. He felt oppressed by the crowd and began thinking he'd lost her for good. A group of women wearing open bodices surrounded him, their bodies dripping with sweat as they shook in a sort of primitive dance. He saw himself as rather grotesque, lost in a ragged crowd wearing a white linen suit. A man wearing a fake beard jumped towards him and stole his panama hat from his head. He stood motionless, petrified. Then, just as quickly as the crowd had assembled, it dispersed. All of a sudden, he caught sight of her, covered in ticker tape, swaying her hips in front of a man playing maracas. He lingered for a while observing the scene, in the middle of that frenzied outburst, keeping his gaze obstinately fixed on his wife. She appeared to be floating before his eyes as if in a dream. He felt a hand on his shoulder.

"It's about time, there you are!" Koogan exclaimed. "You had us frightened out of our wits… but isn't Lotte with you?"

He pointed to his wife with his index finger.

A grand ball was being held at the Teatro Municipal. Koogan promised that they would amuse themselves there. Champagne would flow like water. Ray Ventura's Orchestra was scheduled to perform. They headed to the Teatro. The ball was to be held in the great hall, which was situated on the main floor. It was an altogether different atmosphere, devoid of cross-dressing men and buxom women covered in glitter. This was where the white people had fun. Men wore dinner jackets and women were attired in sumptuous gowns. Nevertheless, the atmosphere was still suffused with a certain madness and abandon. Men and women were swaying their hips in the mirror-panelled rooms, stamping their feet to the rhythm of sambas played by the orchestra. People formed into conga lines that snaked through the hall, and then broke off to mingle once more in that contagious frenzy. Confetti rained down and camera bulbs flashed. Stefan had never witnessed such anarchy before. He drained the champagne flutes he was offered, and let the spectacle of beautiful women go to his head, then went for a walk around the room. The night seemed to last for ever. Everything in the room—the fabrics, the tables, the marble—seemed suffused with a drunken perfume. This new smell seemed to augur a fresh start. Perhaps tomorrow wouldn't herald the end of the world. The singing in the room was imbued with a genuine sense of brotherhood. A new humanity was being built in the streets and palaces. The orchestra began playing a slow waltz. Lotte stationed herself in front of him. He uncrossed his arms and grabbed her by the waist. They began to dance. Everything started spinning around them. They picked up the pace and looked grandiose amidst all the other couples. On they danced, ignoring everyone around them, ignoring the past, ignoring the future. Looking right into her eyes, he told her he loved her. She held his gaze, then brought her lips to his ear and explained that she hadn't understood what he'd said over all that noise. Could he repeat it?

"I love you," he said once more.

Outside, the night was slowly turning to dawn.

Tuesday, 17th February, in the morning.

They walked in single file on the pavement under the scorching sun. They entered the crowds that had assembled once more on the streets to celebrate Mardi Gras, a crowd that was still drunk on the excesses of the previous night's festivities, and exhilarated by the day's prospects. They marched ahead, their heads hung low, through the deafening din as drums were pounded, fireworks exploded and whistles were blown. They didn't talk. He wore black velvet trousers and a slightly creased shirt, while she was wearing a shapeless grey dress. They were carrying a suitcase each. He was leading the way. He was forced to confront people's wrathful stares as he pushed past them. He didn't excuse himself. No words left his mouth. His lips were dry. He tried to get his bearings as he walked in the direction of Praça Mauá, where they would take the bus back to Petrópolis. Lotte followed him closely, terrified at the thought that she might lose him. They walked through the street party as it rose from the ashes of the previous day, sustained by the exuberance of the night's festivities. A man in a clown's costume strode up to Lotte and started gesticulating. She walked past him unheedingly. A woman behind her showered her with insults and pushed her. Lotte lost her balance. Her suitcase snapped open and spilt its contents on the ground. Lotte shouted to draw her husband's attention. He heard her cry amidst the uproar. He turned around and headed back towards her. She put her belongings back in the suitcase one by one. The woman who had insulted her grabbed Lotte's red dress off the ground, held it out at arm's length, tossed it on the asphalt and carried on dancing. Laughter burst out all around her. Lotte's eyes welled with tears. Stefan closed the suitcase. Frozen with fear, she stared at her dress as it got trampled by the crowd. Stefan urged her to hurry up. She followed him. They drew near the bus station. Stefan had now got his bearings and knew where he was going. They came across a tram chock-full of people dancing to the sound of a little orchestra. They slipped through a crowd that refused to make way for them. They fled Rio. They followed their shadows as they stretched out on the ground. The fever that was gripping the city no longer affected them. Their hearts were frozen in fear. Their eyes saw abysses opening up all around them. They were immune to the warmth of the flares being lit all around them. They marched on, enveloped in their pain. The windows of buildings gleamed in the sun. Yet their eyes registered nothing but hailstorms and cold, wretched, endless rains. They were going back to their tomb. They were starting back for Petrópolis on that festive day in which they'd placed so many of their hopes. Tomorrow would be Ash Wednesday. As far as they were concerned, it was already Ash Wednesday. They had seen the newspaper headlines that morning. Singapore had fallen. Singapore, the last remaining bastion of civilization, had surrendered to the Japanese. They hadn't seen it coming. The impregnable British fortress and its hundred thousand soldiers! The headline had read: "THE BRITISH HAVE LOST THE WAR." The last bastion had fallen. The barbarians had the world at their feet. Nothing could ever stop them now. Henceforth, His Majesty's soldiers would march through the Malaysian jungle with their heads hung low. Singapore had fallen. The Japanese had secured their oil supplies. The war was over. The Germans were advancing towards Suez. Any day now, the Axis Powers would be able to combine their forces. In a year's time, the barbarians would arrive in Rio. The party was over. There was no sanctuary left, nowhere left to hide. Their faces were etched with pain and suffering. If Singapore had fallen, there was no army or general on earth that could withstand the waves of enemy soldiers. It was time to stop hoping for a better tomorrow. It was time to admit defeat. The dreaded moment had finally come to pass. They could no longer aspire to peace and happiness. There would be no world of tomorrow and the world of yesterday had disappeared. The years of terror had gone on long enough. The sham of a life they had lived had backfired. It was time to rejoin their people, to follow in their footsteps, the path ahead of them had already been mapped.

They left Cláudio de Souza and the other Koogans behind. They left their grotesque illusions behind in Rio. They felt guilty. They had behaved disgracefully. They had laughed, sung and danced. Luckily, Singapore, the martyred city, had reawoken them to the bleak state of affairs. The crowds around them had no idea of the catastrophe about to befall them. Their drunken, bloodshot eyes were blind. Those happy, simple souls were dancing on the ruins of Singapore. They went about in the grips of ecstasy while the *danse macabre* was readying to bear down on them. There would never be an end to the misery.

There was nothing to keep them perched on the brink of the abyss. It was time to leave this world. To go back to Petrópolis.

They had dismissed the housekeeper. The gardener had taken Sunday off. The house was bathed in light. Birdsong filtered through the half-open windows and the gently swaying curtains. They paced around their house for one last time. Everything was neat and tidy. The letters they had written over the past week had been carefully arranged on the little desk. They had spent Wednesday, Thursday, Friday and Saturday dedicated to that single task. One letter was destined for Abrahão Koogan, while others had been written to Victor Wittkowski, Lotte's brother and Friderike's brother, while he'd reserved the longest for his dear friend Jules Romains Sunday morning had been set aside to write a statement intended for their Brazilian hosts, and the last letter he'd composed, just an hour earlier, had been addressed to Friderike. He had drafted those letters with the same dedication with which he'd worked on his books. He had chosen his words carefully to avoid wounding the letters' recipients and to ensure they knew how dearly they've been loved. The same man who'd never been one for pouring his heart out had allowed the letters' recipients to read the intensity of his emotions, friendship and love between the lines. Though he was under no illusions, he'd tried his best to explain his actions. Who would understand or forgive him? Only Friderike might grasp the meaning of his act. She was the only one who had ever glimpsed into the recesses of his tormented soul.

They had stayed up late the previous night. Feder and his wife had come to dinner. It had been a delightful evening. They had talked about literature, Goethe, his *Wilhelm Meister*, which Stefan had just finished reading—and which in the end he'd found so woolly and stiff when compared to *Werther*. On that point, they had agreed. Before the Feders had taken their leave, Stefan had suggested he and Feder play a game of chess. Needless to say, Stefan had lost. He had detected surprise in Feder's eyes when he'd returned the books he'd recently borrowed from him.

"You've already read them?"

His eyes would never settle on a page again, there would be no more reading. Never again would his eyes glimpse into another world. Never again would he experience the strange and brilliant sensation of being sucked into an author's universe, never again would he voyage through his imagination while time stood still. Never again would he experience the euphoria of writing, or taste the morsels of valour and passionate love, or unveil the magical secrets of wordplay. Life had only been bearable when ensconced in his world of words. Turning pages or writing in them had been the only act in his life that had come effortlessly to him. He had never been able to interact with people in an equally carefree way. Luckily, the final curtain had fallen. He had finished performing in his human comedy, he was done playing the role of Stefan Zweig.

· Plucki, his adorable fox terrier, came to lick his hand. Stefan stroked him, kissed his snout and let him out into the garden to play. The house had to be empty. The dog ran outside, barking. Would Margarida Banfield look after him properly? In his letter, Stefan had asked her to do so as a personal favour. Seeing as how he had leased the bungalow until the beginning of April, he had also slipped enough money to cover the rent for March in the same envelope. He didn't want to leave any debts. He didn't want to cause anyone the slightest inconvenience. Still, his act would cast opprobrium on his name until the end of time. One didn't have to be a genius to imagine what people would say about him. That he had abandoned others to their pain and deserted when the time had come to fight the enemy. When others had expected him to be an example, a hero even, he had run off like a coward. They would accuse him of innumerable sins. They would be indignant. At best, they would respond with incomprehension. He pictured Thomas Mann's disdain, Bernanos's rage and Jules Romains's sadness. But the relief he felt welling up in his heart compensated for the shame he felt and swept away all of his scruples. His suffering had come to an end.

He decided to get dressed. He opened his wardrobe and lingered in front of it for a long while, then picked out a dark suit. As it was Sunday, he opted for a sports jacket, a brown short-sleeved shirt, a plain tie and a pair of knickerbockers. He went into the bathroom, carefully shaved himself and combed his hair. Looking at himself in the mirror, he told himself he'd done all he could.

She strolled slowly along Avenida Koeler. She admired the scenes around her, the streets, the landscapes, the faces of passers-by and the sky above her. She walked on, short of breath, exhausted by a sleepless night. Her cheeks were awash with tears, she wanted to drain her body of all its tears, right there and then on the pavement. She had promised him she wouldn't cry in front of him. She had spent the entire morning wandering around the town. Her lips murmured words only she could hear. She prayed to God, the God of Abraham, Isaac and Jacob. She prayed using the few words of Hebrew she still remembered from her childhood, when she had listened, wide-eyed, to her grandfather's booming tenor during the Sabbath evening service. She praised the Lord, her God, the king of all the earth. She peppered her

Hebrew prayer with German in order to give her words some shape and sense. She asked God to forgive her. She begged her brother Manfred to forgive her. She wished Eva a long, happy life and hoped Eva's dreams would remain unblemished by visions of her unhappy aunt. She crossed the bridge that spanned the canal, directed her gaze to the cathedral and begged God for forgiveness once again, the same God that had abandoned the Jews to the hands of the barbarians, the God who had allowed His children to die and left the survivors nothing but a life of sadness and exile. When a passer-by drew near, looking a little puzzled, she dried her tears and looked away to hide her face. From the opposite bank of the Piabanha River, she looked at the Crystal Palace, and pictured herself walking alongside it by her husband's side when they had first arrived in town. She heard the echoes of his beloved voice tell her about the palace's history, the story of the aristocrat who had built that glass monument out of love for his wife, and who had sent to Europe for the iron framework. Although it had only been six months ago, she remembered his voice as sounding happy when he had told her that story, but look at what sort of gift he was offering her now. She had promised she wouldn't cry. She would follow him, just as peacefully and joyfully as she had strolled arm in arm with him through the city's streets. Clutching his shoulder, she would go with him into the dark unknown from which there would be no return. She made a detour through the market. The greengrocers were arranging their produce on their stalls, touting their fruit and vegetables, are you not buying anything today, Mrs Zweig? Look at those guavas, here you go, they're all yours. She said next time, she would come back tomorrow, or the following Sunday. But she would never come back, she would never again watch the wonderful spectacle as the sun set over the city, she would never again feel her heart fill with love as he confided in her, or wait to hear a word from him, or experience one of his glances, the delight she felt when he looked at her, or when he whispered words into her ear. She was overwhelmed by all the sights around her. She wanted to take the slightest of the day's wonders with her and carry them for ever in her heart, she wanted her heart to store all the perfumes, scents, the blue of the sky, the green of the forests on the other side of the river, the sing-song of hummingbirds, the cries of children. She wanted to wrap herself in the scalding warmth of the sun as it beat down on the city on that accursed day. She knew she would be cold, that the next world would be enshrouded in night, that she would feel even shorter of breath over there. She looked around with eyes full of sadness and confusion. She longed to cross paths with Feder or his wife, or Mrs Banfield—anyone who would be moved by the sight of a woman in tears and would take her hand and lead her to their home, offer her a drink, give her a bed to sleep in, for just an hour, or maybe even a whole night. Never again would she have to set foot in that houses of ghosts, down there, on 34 Rua Gonçalves Dias. But the streets were empty on that Sunday afternoon under the brutal sun, only a few shadows loomed over the streets, and so she headed back home. The farther she walked, the more she felt as if the sun were already starting to set, the day were growing darker, a cold wind were on the rise. Silence fell all around her. Even the birdsong wasn't as loud as it once was, and her clouded eyes could no longer discern the true brightness of colours.

Meanwhile the house was coming into sight, up there, at the end of a small slope. She climbed the hill, each gulp of air stinging her lungs. She would stop every four or five metres to catch her breath. She would cast her eyes around, but there was nobody coming towards her. One would have thought that the city's inhabitants had simply vanished, or that they'd gone to hide, nobody would come to her aid, nobody would come to rescue her. She could have cried for help, but no words rose out of her mouth. She brought her hand to her eyelids, which were dry. She had cried all the tears out of her body. There she was, standing in front of the door. She lifted her gaze high to the sky, where the sun was shining. She breathed in a deep lungful of clean air, shut her eyelids, murmured one last prayer to the Lord to thank Him for having brought that man into her life, for having allowed her to experience a boundless love for him. For one last time, she begged for forgiveness and murmured: "The Lord gave, and the Lord hath taken away; blessed be the name of the Lord."

Two vials had been prepared and filled to the brim with little white crystals. An empty glass had been placed next to each of the vials and there was a bottle of Salutaris mineral water in the middle, the same natural spring water they'd taken with all their meals—and which would be the last drink they would ever consume together. Drenched in sweat, she had decided to take a bath. Then she had slipped into a flowery dressing gown, which she had worn on evenings when she had wanted to look particularly fetching, just like she did today.

He gazed at her as she came out of the bathroom with a questioning look. She nodded and forced a weak smile. She walked slowly, uncertainly, and went to sit down on the bed beside him. She regretted not having had a drink, that she wasn't drunk, but he'd refused to allow her to do so. He had wanted to be fully conscious in order to experience the moment in serenity. She shuddered. Fear could be read on her features. He drew her closer to him and kissed her tenderly on the lips. He looked long and deep into her eyes. "I'll go first," he said. "You'll follow me... if that's what you want." She couldn't hold back her tears. He reminded her of the promise she'd made him. She apologized. Her sobs swelled in her chest. He dried her cheeks. He kissed her eyelids. He whispered words into her ear that were meant to dispel her fear. He stood up and walked over to the dresser where the vials had been placed. He turned back to look at her, as if wanting to read approval in her eyes. She held back a scream. She would have loved to rush towards him, spill the vials and run out of the house, but it was as if she were hypnotized by his stare, as if the poison had already had its effect. He had kept his composure and seemed at peace. He picked up the first vial and with untrembling fingers tipped its contents into the glass. Then he filled the glass with mineral water. He turned around to face her once more. She was silent and still. From the depths of her despair, she stared at him, terrified. She managed to form a sentence. Did he love her? He said that he did. She found the strength to come and stand by his side. She tried to mimic his gestures, but when she'd taken hold of the vial, she almost spilt its contents. He calmly took hold of her hand. He filled her glass.

There they stood, facing one another, looking into one another's eyes. He raised the glass to his lips without removing his gaze from her. He drained the glass in three gulps without stopping for breath. He said he was going to lie down. That she should join him when she was ready. He stretched out on the bed. She drank, quickly, and then ran after him to be by his side, clinging to his shoulder.

He breathed in her body's heady scent. He asked her if she needed anything. She wasn't able to answer him. Her tears were preventing her from seeing anything, but was there anything to see? He said that a thousand things were crowding his mind. Off in the distance, they perceived the fantastic landscape of a familiar world, a European city with brightly lit pavements, where he recognized many faces and people embraced him. He said that everything was slowly growing darker. What about her, what was she seeing? She didn't reply. He said that everything was blending together, the past, the present, lights were becoming confused and that he was in a hall plunged in semi-darkness. He recognized a familiar silhouette that brushed past him, the silhouette of a woman, with a fan in her hand and a haughty expression, walking along a corridor. He carried on talking, but the words no longer formed properly in his mouth. She kissed his forehead and his eyelids. His eyelids were shut. He could no longer see or hear anything. She kissed his temples. Although her lips had met his skin, she could no longer feel its warmth. Her own lips had grown cold. She stretched out her arms towards him, but they were as frozen as though they'd been plunged into ice. Her fingertips grazed his shoulder, but her arms grew heavy. Her strength was abandoning her. He was out of reach and out of sight. Her eyes could distinguish the outlines of a shadow beside her. The shadow drifted away into the darkness and faded into the netherworld. Day turned to night. The earth was shapeless and empty. She joined him in the abyss, and a gust of wind that came through the open windows shook the curtains and hovered over that abyss.

This novel is based on facts and historical events culled from various archives, witness accounts and documents. The remarks and reflections made by some characters are faithfully based on the books, articles and correspondence these characters left behind.

Here is a partial bibliography of the sources used during the writing of this novel:

Hannah Arendt, "Stefan Zweig: Jews in the World of Yesterday", in *Reflections on Literature and Culture*, Stanford University Press, 2007.

Georges Bernanos, *Brésil, terre d'amitié*, La Table Ronde, 2009.

George Clare, *Last Waltz in Vienna*, Pan Macmillan, 2002.

Robert Dumont, *Stefan Zweig et la France*, Didier, 1967.

William M. Johnston, *The Austrian Mind*, University of California Press, 1992.

Sébastien Lapaque, *Sous le soleil de l'exil, Georges Bernanos au Brésil*, Grasset, 2003.

Klaus Mann, *The Turning Point*, Markus Wiener, 1995.

Serge Niémetz, *Stefan Zweig, Le Voyageur et ses mondes*, Belfond, 1999.

Donald A. Prater, *European of Yesterday*, Clarendon Press, 1972.

Arthur Schnitzler, *My Youth in Vienna*, Weidenfeld & Nicolson, 1971.

Friderike and Stefan Zweig, *L'Amour inquiet*, Éditions des Femmes, 1987.

Stefan Zweig, *Journaux (1912–1940)*, Belfond, 1986.

Stefan Zweig, *Œuvre complète*, La Pochothèque, 3 vols, Le Livre de Poche, 2001.

Stefan Zweig, *Correspondances*, 3 vols (1897–1919; 1920–31; 1932–42), Grasset, 2008.

Stefan Zweig, *The World of Yesterday*, Pushkin Press, 2009.

QUOTATIONS

p. 50   "So I ask my memories to speak and choose for me, and give at least some faint reflection of my life before it sinks into the dark."

From Stefan Zweig, *The World of Yesterday*, trans. Anthea Bell (London: Pushkin Press, 2009), p. 22.

p. 102   "He may not sleep who watches over the people. The Lord hath appointed me to watch and to give warning."

From Stefan Zweig, *Jeremiah: A Drama in Nine Scenes*, trans. Eden and Cedar Paul (New York, NY: Thomas Seltzer, 1922), p. 216.

p. 102   "Wanderers, sufferers, our drink must be drawn from distant waters, evil their taste, bitter in the mouth, the nations will drive us from home after home, we will wander down suffering's endless roads, eternally vanquished, thralls at the hearths where in passing we rest."

From Stefan Zweig, *Jeremiah: A Drama in Nine Scenes*, trans. Eden and Cedar Paul (New York, NY: Thomas Seltzer, 1922), pp. 331–35.

p. 120   "And their fear of death turns to hopeless resignation."

From Stefan Zweig, "In the Snow", *Wondrak and Other Stories*, trans. Anthea Bell (London: Pushkin Press, 2009), p. 25.

p. 120   "Josua holds his fiancée with cold hands. She is dead already, although he does not know it."

From Stefan Zweig, "In the Snow", *Wondrak and Other Stories*, trans. Anthea Bell (London: Pushkin Press, 2009), p. 24.

p. 124   "My heart is so sore, that I might almost say the daylight hurts my nose whenever I stick it out of the window."

From Stefan Zweig, *The Struggle with the Daemon*, trans. Eden and Cedar Paul (London: Pushkin Press, 2012), p. 222.

p. 128   "...left Marie von Kleist, who was also dear to him, in loneliness and neglect; and dragged Henriette Vogel down with him to death... he retired more and more into himself, growing more solitary even than nature had created him."

From Stefan Zweig, *The Struggle with the Daemon*, trans. Eden and Cedar Paul (London: Pushkin Press, 2012), pp. 162–63.

p. 128   "Like every other of his hyperbolical affects, Kleist's passion for a fellowship on which a joint suicide could alone put the seal remained a mystery to his friends. Vainly did he seek a companion into the Valley of the Shadow. One and all they contemptuously or shudderingly rejected the proposal."

From Stefan Zweig, *The Struggle with the Daemon*, trans. Eden and Cedar Paul (London: Pushkin Press, 2012), p. 225.

p. 128   "He encountered a woman, hitherto almost a stranger, who thanked him for his strange invitation. She was an invalid, whose death could not in any case be long delayed, for her body was inwardly devoured by cancer even as Kleist's mind was devoured by weariness of life. Though herself incapable of forming a vigorous resolution, she was sensitive and highly suggestible, and therefore open to the promptings of his morbid enthusiasm; she agreed to plunge with him into the unknown."

From Stefan Zweig, *The Struggle with the Daemon*, trans. Eden and Cedar Paul (London: Pushkin Press, 2012), p. 225.

p. 129   "At bottom this somewhat priggish and sentimental wife of a tax-collector was of a type uncongenial to Kleist... She who would have been too petty, too soft, too weak for him as a living companion, was welcomed by him as a comrade in death."

From Stefan Zweig, *The Struggle with the Daemon*, trans. Eden and Cedar Paul (London: Pushkin Press, 2012), p. 226.

p. 129   "Although another woman swore to be his companion in death, his thoughts turned to her for whom he had lived and whom he loved, to Marie von Kleist."

From Stefan Zweig, *The Struggle with the Daemon*, trans. Eden and Cedar Paul (London: Pushkin Press, 2012), p. 230.

p. 129   "In the high spirits of honeymooners, the couple drive to the Wannsee. The host at the inn hears them laughing, sees them sporting merrily in the fields, can tell how they drank their coffee with gusto in the open air. Then, at the prearranged hour, came the two pistol shots, in swift succession, the first that with which Kleist pierced his companion's heart, the second that with which (barrel in mouth) he blew out his own brains. His hand did not falter. It was true that he knew better how to die than to live."

From Stefan Zweig, *The Struggle with the Daemon*, trans. Eden and Cedar Paul (London: Pushkin Press, 2012), p. 232.

p. 130   "You beam through the blindfold covering my eyes
At me with the radiance of a thousand suns.
Wings have put forth on both my shoulders,
My spirit lifts through the ether's silent spaces."

From Heinrich von Kleist, *Selected Writings of Heinrich von Kleist*, trans. David Constantine (Indianapolis, IN, and Cambridge, MA: Hackett, 2004), p. 204.

PUSHKIN PRESS

Pushkin Press was founded in 1997. Having first rediscovered European classics of the twentieth century, Pushkin now publishes novels, essays, memoirs, children's books, and everything from timeless classics to the urgent and contemporary.

Pushkin Paper books, like this one, represent exciting, high-quality writing from around the world. Pushkin publishes widely acclaimed, brilliant authors such as Stefan Zweig, Marcel Aymé, Antal Szerb, Paul Morand and Yasushi Inoue, as well as some of the most exciting contemporary and often prize-winning writers, including Andrés Neuman, Edith Pearlman and Ryu Murakami.

Pushkin Press publishes the world's best stories, to be read and read again.

*